THE VIPER'S HEAD

ANNA MCCLUSKEY

Book 2 of the Mathilda Holiday Series

Author website: **www.theannafiles.com**
BookBub: **www.bookbub.com/profile/anna-mccluskey**
Facebook: **www.facebook.com/annamccluskeyauthor**

Cover art by Sleepy Fox Studios
www.sleepyfoxstudios.net

Dedicated in memory of

Daniel Hamm,

who would not have read it,

but who made great toasted ravioli

and played a mean blues guitar.

1.

"I'm so sorry for your loss," murmured yet another black-clad stranger standing in front of Mattie. She stifled a yawn and resisted the urge to glance at the clock, instead nodding somberly, her face frozen in a plastered-on look of grief.

This fake funeral had been dragging on for ages. As the mourners moved on to speak to her friend Trevor – who had been her sister's best friend since they were eight and who at least seemed to know who the hell they were – Mattie finally allowed herself to peek up at the ornate grandfather clock across the room. It had been two hours, and the wake was set to go for one more.

"We should have done a happy hour thing instead," she muttered to Ida, who was just sidling up beside her. "At least then I wouldn't be choking on the smell of all these flowers."

Ida was one of the few people who knew that Mattie's identical twin sister, Tillie, was actually still alive.

"Is a happy hour appropriate for a wake?" Ida raised an iron-grey eyebrow. "Funerals are for being sad, I always say."

"Well, you know, these days, sometimes you do more of a celebration of the person's life," said Mattie, uncertainly. "We could have done that." She eyed the sad buffet table adorned with a couple of uninspired cheese plates. "With better food, maybe."

"Too late now, I suppose," said Ida, cheerfully.

Mattie laughed. Ida was Trevor's next-door neighbor and while she was every day of eighty, she was still sharp as a tack.

She was also one of the first mages they had stumbled upon when they had discovered this new world of magic, and she had good reason to want to help them against the Auditors – she'd lost three family members to their scheming herself.

Speaking of which…. Mattie's eyes narrowed as a new guest entered the funeral home. He wasn't much to look at. With his sandy blond hair, bland smile, and the same beige suit he always wore – he must have a closet full of them – he blended right into the surroundings. Mattie suspected he cultivated that banality.

Beside her, Ida gasped softly. Mattie and Trevor had told her that they had encountered her nephew, but this would be the first time she'd seen him since he was kidnapped by the Auditors fifteen years ago.

It was also the first time Mattie had seen him since he'd disappeared after saving their lives in that last mage battle in Seattle. She wondered how he'd known about the funeral and why he'd decided this was an appropriate time to make his appearance. Granted, he knew as well as she did that the funeral was a sham, but it still seemed in poor taste to show up uninvited to a wake.

And she still wasn't sure she trusted him.

Mattie strode toward the door, grabbing Giovani Garavedi by the arm and hauling him off to the side into a discreet alcove. She pushed him over to a floral-patterned divan.

He sat down and looked up at her, one eyebrow raised, a small smile playing on his lips.

Mattie frowned. What was he looking so amused about? "What are you doing here?" she hissed.

She sensed someone behind her, and she whirled around. It was only Trevor and Ida. Mattie relaxed slightly and stepped aside to make room for them in the tight space.

Ida still looked shocked. She walked forward slowly, as though in a daze, then knelt in front of her nephew, reaching out one hand as though to touch his face, but stopping just short of doing so, her hand in its black lace glove hovering inches away from him. "Giovani?" she whispered.

"Giovani," he repeated. His smile had faded and he looked sad. "No one has called me Giovani in years, Auntie Ida."

Mattie raised her eyebrows. It was odd to hear the childish moniker from an adult, especially from someone she had seen as a spy and a warrior.

Then again, people were people, and people were complicated.

Ida looked into his eyes, finally cupping his smooth cheek in her gloved hand. "I can't say that you were ever my favorite, but I was sorry to see you gone, and I'm glad you're back. You've lost your innocence, I suppose. I hope you've gained some wisdom."

A tear rolled down his face, stopped by Ida's finger. "I think I have, Auntie."

Mattie felt a nudge and tore her eyes away from the reunion scene to find Trevor gesturing with his head back toward the main party.

Reluctantly, she followed him.

"I felt sort of intrusive, you know?" he murmured to her once they were away.

"Yeah, but I want to know what's happening," she pointed out. "And why he's here. And what he wants. And what Ida's saying to him."

Trevor's lips twitched. "I'm sure Ida will tell us all about it later. Right now, you've got mingling to do. And look sad! We need to be convincing."

"Fine." Mattie looked around, hoping for someone else she knew, but the room was full of strangers. The fact was that she and Tillie had had a mainly phone-based relationship for the past eighteen years, ever since their parents had died.

Mattie had fled, unable to cope, citing better college programs as her reason. Tillie had stayed behind and their lives had gone in very different directions.

Mattie had never been a part of Tillie's life in St. Louis, and she'd been giving some serious consideration to sticking around this time. The life she'd built for herself in Portland had tumbled to the ground – she was in the middle of a divorce, had quit her job, lost her apartment. And now, having "inherited" Tillie's condo, she could start over.

But she still didn't know who any of these people were – people who considered themselves close enough to Tillie to mourn her passing.

She glanced back over at Giovani and Ida and was surprised to see that another mourner had joined them. Mattie glanced at Trevor, planning to ask if he knew the man, but her friend was already engrossed in conversation with a beautiful Asian woman in an elegant blue cocktail dress.

Mattie returned her focus to the trio in the alcove near the door. She inched her way along the wall toward them, fingers sliding over the textured wallpaper as she skulked along, curious and hoping to unobtrusively overhear something. Maybe this was another member of the Garaveldi family?

She peeked around the corner into the alcove and saw the man push his glowing hands forward and Giovani slam back into the wall.

Probably not a relative, then, or at least not a friendly one.

She rushed forward into the alcove just in time, as Ida erected a shimmering shield spell in the doorway, hiding them from the rest of the funeral.

Mattie tackled the newcomer, and the two of them crashed to the ground, narrowly missing Giovani's feet.

She pushed herself up on her arms, and as soon as she untangled her limbs from his, Ida and Giovani began throwing magical attacks his way.

The man threw up a shield of his own and angrily shoved Mattie away. He scrambled to his feet, reaching toward Giovani once again.

Focusing all her energy, Mattie whispered, "Stumble and bumble, you clumsy oaf."

Mattie's hands glowed and the man tripped over a corresponding glow on the floor, tumbling to his knees.

"Where is she?" he shouted up at Giovani. "Where's Agent Miller, you fucking snake?"

Oh, shit. This was another Auditor, one of Giovani's former associates and a member of the secret society that had tried to kidnap Tillie.

Mattie hoped Ida's spell was sound-proof as well as camouflaging.

"How would I know?" Giovani raised an eyebrow and calmly settled his jacket back into place, adjusting the cuffs and smoothing down the lapels. "Didn't she scamper back to HQ like a good little agent after her successful mission?"

Mattie frowned. Agent Miller was dead. What was Giovani talking about?

Then it dawned on her. She had spelled Agent Miller's body to look like Tillie. That was the whole reason they were having this sham funeral.

She glanced involuntarily toward the front of the room, where an urn was displayed, surrounded by gigantic floral arrangements. She couldn't actually see it through the blur of Ida's shield, but she knew it was there, and she knew it contained Agent Miller's ashes, not Tillie's.

An odd sound filled the alcove and Mattie glanced back toward the arguing mages.

The new agent was hissing. Actually hissing. She'd never heard anyone do that before, and she watched with interest as his face turned bright red and he clenched and unclenched his fists.

Finally, he clamped his lips shut and the sound ceased. He inhaled sharply and visibly collected himself, drawing himself back up to his feet.

"This is all very unprofessional," said Giovani, before the man could speak again. "If I didn't know better, I would guess that you weren't sent here. I would wonder, in fact, if you were acting outside of the organization's instructions." He paused. "Or even, dare I think it, *against* their instructions?" He shook his head. "No, of course not. An agent in such good standing as you would never do such a thing."

The man pursed his lips and stepped back, stumbling against the wall.

"But then again," Giovani continued. "You do seem to be alone." He took a step forward. "Without your partner." He stepped forward again and leaned toward the man, lowering his voice and speaking directly into his ear.

Mattie strained to hear.

"It all seems very contrary to standard protocol."

The Auditor slumped. He seemed defeated. "Yes, fine, you bastard. I came alone. I came against orders." He straightened and narrowed his eyes at Giovani. "But I know you're behind this. You backslid. You're an abomination and I know you kidnapped Agent Miller. I will find her and free her and we will come for you and your friends. You can't hide forever."

Giovani smiled slightly. "I am an excellent hider, Agent Parker." He nodded toward Ida, who lowered her shield and pushed a glowing hand toward Agent Parker.

He lurched as though shoved and spun around toward the funeral home door, lumbering forward until he reached it. It opened of its own accord and he fell through it. Ida slammed it behind him with a flourish and the glow around her hands faded.

"What an unpleasant person," she remarked. "Giovani, I hope you're finished hanging around those

Auditors. You can't be too careful about whose company you keep, I always say."

He was silent, and Mattie crossed her arms, leveling a stare at him. "You are finished with them, aren't you?"

Giovani went pale and he wobbled toward a sofa a few paces away, collapsing onto it.

Mattie frowned, startled again. What was going on here? Giovani had always seemed completely unflappable.

"I'll get you some tea," said Ida. She strode away.

Crouching in front of Giovani, Mattie peered into his face. "It feels like you're overreacting. What am I missing? You were super calm just a moment ago."

He nodded. He took in a long, ragged breath before finally speaking. "I'm good under pressure. Once the pressure's gone, I tend to deflate. You've only seen me in the pressure cooker, but if we're going to work together, you'll see me like this a lot."

"Fair enough." Mattie nodded. "So, you're okay? Just catch your breath."

"Here's the thing, though," he continued. His breathing was beginning to even out, his voice growing thoughtful. "That was really fucking weird."

"It didn't seem that weird to me," said Mattie. "It seemed like something we should have been prepared for. How did none of us think about the fact that the Auditors would come looking for their missing agent?"

Giovani chuckled weakly, closing his light brown eyes and shaking his head. "That wasn't 'the Auditors.' That was a rogue agent."

Mattie's legs began to cramp, so she moved to a seat beside Giovani on the couch. Her brow furrowed in puzzlement. "A rogue agent? Like you?"

"Not like me." He sighed. "Apparently agents are going rogue in various ways now."

Ida returned balancing three steaming white mugs on a tray. She set it down on a table beside the couch, edging aside a vase of white silk flowers. "I figured we could all use some tea," she said.

"Always," said Mattie, accepting her mug with a smile. She wrapped her hands around it, the warmth comforting and familiar, and breathed in the fragrant steam.

"Now," said Ida, briskly. "What was that all about?"

"Apparently the Auditors are all going rogue," said Mattie. She took a sip. It was some kind of green tea, with a delightful nuttiness to it.

"No, no," said Giovani. "Not all of them. Probably. Just me and Parker. The question is why Parker was here."

"Wasn't he looking for Agent Miller?" Ida raised her formidable eyebrows. "Seems pretty simple to me. They were friends, I suppose. Or lovers, maybe."

Giovani shook his head. "I never heard that they were. Lovers, I mean. I guess they could have been friends, but it still doesn't explain why he would be looking for her. It's just not how we – they – do things."

"Maybe they were secret lovers," Mattie suggested. "I bet that kind of thing is frowned on, right?

"What kind of thing?" Giovani frowned.

"You know. . . . inter-agent canoodling?"

"On the contrary." He paused, sipping his tea. "While we didn't often have time for relationships, reproduction among agents is encouraged. Got to fill the court somehow."

"The court?" said Mattie. "Like a court of law?"

He shook his head. "More like a royal court."

"And all the courtiers are the children of Auditors?"

Giovani rubbed his forehead. "It's more complicated than that. We're talking about an ancient society that operates completely outside of regular society, made up of people who are fanatical about protecting it and equally fanatical about their mission to bring balance to the rest of the world."

Trevor appeared in the doorway. "Mattie! What the hell? I've been looking for you. You have to be out here, mingling, mourning, making this look real. I can't hold up this funeral by myself."

"Right!" she jumped to her feet. "Let's just table this whole rogue Auditor situation for now. Maybe we could meet up later and discuss it?"

Ida nodded. "Of course, dear. You've got to do your duty by your sister, I suppose. Family first, I always say."

Reluctantly, Mattie followed Trevor back into the room full of strangers who knew her twin and thought she was dead.

2.

Bored, Tillie tossed aside her magazine with a frustrated sigh. She missed the coffee table, and it landed on the hardwood floor, its glossy pages falling open to a picture of the smiling royal family of some European nation.

A small ironic smile hovered on her lips as she leaned forward to study their elegant visages. They were irrelevant in these modern times. Like her – dead, but still hanging around.

She shook her head and snatched up the magazine once again, placing it carefully back on the table where it belonged. She might technically be dead, but she refused to be irrelevant.

Tillie stood and stretched to her full five feet two inches, lifting her arms over her head. She moved gracefully into a yogic mountain pose, closing her eyes and breathing deeply. She slid her left foot outward, instinctively pivoting as she did so to avoid stubbing her toe on the table. Bending her knee and lowering her arms to stretch to either side, she sank into a warrior two pose. She twisted her head to gaze over her forward hand and held the pose for several breaths before smoothly lifting back up and then folding into a wide-legged downward dog, deftly rolling the coffee table on its castors forward and out of her way.

Moving through vinyasa after vinyasa, Tillie could feel herself growing calmer and more serene. So what if she was trapped in her condo? Her condo was a haven, one she had spent years perfecting. Each element within this gorgeous space was either hand-picked or a well-loved family piece that she had chosen to preserve.

And she was a seer. If she had to be trapped, at least her main magical talent lay in seeing the future or scrying to see the outside world. A speller, who could only do spells affecting what was present, or a stitcher, who used gestures to manipulate space and time, would be truly trapped.

She could go outside anytime she wanted, without actually leaving. She had a scrying bowl, a crystal ball, and a laptop with the Internet. What more could she want? Adventure? Sure. Yes. She definitely wanted adventure.

Tillie felt her tranquility slipping and she deliberately returned her focus to her yoga practice. She moved into tree pose, which required all of her concentration and balance, breathing in. And out. In. And out. Her heart filled with joy as she held the difficult pose for breath after breath.

She lowered her foot with an exhale. Inhaling, she brought her arms up over her head and then as she exhaled, lowered them to her chest, bringing her other foot up. As she held tree pose again on this side, a scratching sound drifted into her consciousness.

Her pose wavered as part of her mind tried to discern its source. It wasn't coming from the direction of Max's scratching post, and he was usually so good about only scratching that. He better not be destroying anything.

Tillie realized that the sound was coming from the hallway outside the condo. Not the cat, then – probably just a neighbor going about their business. She returned her focus to her practice and her feeling of rootedness strengthened along with her balance.

Then her front door opened and she lost her balance completely as an unfamiliar voice behind her said, "What the fuck?"

Bracing herself on the couch behind her, Tillie spun around to find a furious man glaring at her. He was furious? He was the one breaking into her damn condo!

His hands began to glow, and Tillie hastily muttered some Latin words under her breath, erecting a mage shield.

The man's anger grew and he stepped toward her, flinging lightning bolts from his luminous fingertips. "Abomination!" he shrieked.

Tillie could feel energy draining from her and she banished the shield spell, switching to seer mode instead so she could simply dodge the man's attack spells. "Who the hell–" She dodged a lightning bolt. "Are you?"

"You're supposed to be dead," he informed her through gritted teeth.

"It is very rude to ignore someone's perfectly reasonable question," she pointed out, landing a bare-footed kick on his belly. Tillie danced back as the speller aimed another bolt at the space she had occupied just a moment before.

"I'm your worst fucking nightmare." The man changed his tactics, erecting magical barriers around Tillie, leaving only the path between himself and her open.

Tillie smiled at him. "That's funny. You don't look like a giant crocodile who lives in a tower."

He paused. "That's your worst nightmare?"

She shrugged. "I used to have that dream when I was a kid. Haven't really had a nightmare since. The real world is scarier than anything my imagination can come up with."

"Well, then." The speller aimed another lightning bolt down the tunnel he'd created between them. "I'm the scariest thing in the real world."

Tillie ducked before it hit her. No," she said, softly. "You're not."

She danced toward the speller, renewing her krav maga attacks and forcing him back toward an emerald green chair that once belonged to her mother. She muttered her Latin shield spell again, deflecting his lightning as he collapsed backward into the chair.

Then, with great effort, she moved her hands in a simple stitching motion, and a ball of yarn from Mattie's knitting basket beside the chair moved instantly to tie the spellers arms to the chair, wrapping itself around his fists so that he could no longer direct his lightning bolts toward her.

Her seer senses alerted her that help was on its way, and she beckoned to her neighbor, Scott, as he entered her condo. "Hey, I could use some help keeping this bastard contained."

Scott shut the door behind him and hurried forward, extending his glowing hands and erecting a series of reflective barriers around the glaring intruder.

The other speller's powers dampened and the barriers around Tillie faded away. She took a grateful step back and returned her sight to real-time. "Thanks," she said.

Scott nodded. "Anytime. What are neighbors for? Glad to see you're not actually dead. Want to fill me in on what the hell is going on?"

"She's an abomination," hissed the intruder from the chair.

Tillie rolled her eyes. Not this again. "You're a brainwashed goon," she told him.

Scott emitted a low whistle. "So, the Auditors really are real and they really were after you."

"Apparently they still are," she corrected him. "They don't like it when mages try to learn new disciplines. I'm a seer who was learning to spell and stitch, and they came after me. We thought faking my death would work, but here we are."

"What are we going to do with him?" said Scott.

"There are a few options," Tillie observed, cocking her head as she regarded the captive Auditor. "We could let him go. I'm not really inclined toward that one, but of course, we have to examine all possible outcomes. If we were to let you go, what would you do?"

The man scowled at her. "I'd keep coming after you until you were actually dead."

She tsked. "Not a great answer. Not a compelling argument toward the outcome you probably most want."

"Fanatics don't tend to be super logical," Scott observed. "What's the next option?"

She paced the room. "We could kill him. I'm not really a fan of that one either, actually. I don't have a problem killing in combat, but tying someone up and then slitting his throat doesn't seem very ethical."

Scott nodded. "Absolutely a last resort."

"Interrogation has a certain appeal," Tillie observed. "Find out more about these Auditors, especially since Giovani, the inside man we did have, hasn't been around for a few days." She paused. "Then we'd still have the issue of what to do with him afterward."

She crouched in front of the man and ran her fingers along his chin. "What do you think, Scott?" she said. She looked into the man's eyes as she addressed her neighbor. "Do you think you could torture someone?"

"Probably," Scott said, cheerfully. "I'm not that squeamish. Won't know until we try."

The speller squirmed, and Tillie suppressed a smile. Scott was playing along nicely. And the crack about not being squeamish was particularly good – she had been called over many times to remove spiders for her gentle neighbor.

Hopefully, the threat of torture would be enough to make the Auditor sing. She might be less squeamish than Scott, but torture was not in her wheelhouse, and she didn't intend to add it. But the world of magery was a brutal one, and she knew that a lot of mages wouldn't even hesitate.

She was banking on that fact bolstering her bluff.

"I'm not afraid of you," said the Auditor, but his voice was less steady.

Tillie's smile widened. "Not yet," she said. She stood up and addressed Scott again. "What do you think we'll need? I have some excellent knives in the kitchen, of course."

He pursed his lips in thought. "How about a lighter? I think hot knives work best, don't they?"

"Good point," she said. "And some salt to rub into the cuts?"

"An excellent start," he agreed. "Hopefully, since we're so new at this, we don't cause any irreparable damage."

Turning on her heel, Tillie strode into the kitchen, followed closely by Scott. "I'm not too worried about that," she called over her shoulder. "I mean, he's an Auditor. Who cares how damaged he gets?"

Once in the kitchen, she and Scott exchanged grins.

"You are an evil, evil woman," he murmured, opening her cupboard and pulling out a bag of kale chips. "Is this your idea of snack food?"

"Yes, that's what evil women eat," she said, keeping her voice low as well. "Didn't you know? How long do you think we should let him stew?"

"A couple of minutes at least," he said. He plunged his hand into the bag and came up with a handful of kale chips.

Tillie wrinkled her nose. "Use a bowl, you barbarian. I don't know where your hands have been." She strode across the kitchen and pulled down an ivory ceramic bowl, relieved her neighbor of the bag, and poured him a modest serving.

Scott nibbled on a crispy leaf. "Hey, these aren't bad."

"I'm so pleased you approve." Tillie grabbed a glass from the cupboard before closing it, and then wandered over to the fridge and poured herself some mineral water from a tall, elegant bottle on the top shelf.

Leaning against the island in the middle of her kitchen she sipped her slightly fizzy water and moved into seer mode, sorting through the most likely events to take place in the next few minutes. She sighed and pulled herself back into real-time.

"Well?" said Scott, setting aside his empty bowl.

She frowned at him. "Did you just inhale those? They're not potato chips. Those are grazing food."

He shrugged. "They were good. I was snacky. What do you see?"

"It's about to get complicated. Mattie, Trevor, and two of the Garaveldi mages are on their way up the stairs." Tillie pursed her lips, thinking furiously. "Maybe you should go and intercept them." She turned on her seer mode again to scan through the possibilities. "Damn! There are too many variables. I think at the very least, you should go and let them know what the situation is, so they don't burst in and ruin everything."

Scott nodded. "I can do that. What do I tell Mr. Secret Agent out there about why I'm leaving?"

"Don't tell him anything," Tillie suggested. "Let him wonder."

"Evil, evil woman." Scott chuckled and sauntered back out into the living room.

Tillie peeked around the doorway. "Hurry back!" she called after him.

The Auditor watched Scott go, a wary look on his face.

Smiling slightly, Tillie sashayed toward her prisoner. "Don't worry, honey. We're just gathering a few more supplies. Have you thought at all about what you'd like to tell us? Why you're here? What the Auditors know about me? Where you all hang out? What happens to the people you kidnap?"

A fanatical light filled the man's eyes. "We don't kidnap anyone. We save them."

"Oh, really?" Tillie cocked her head. "Save them from what, exactly?"

"From themselves," he said. "Abominations like you, who have no idea what harm you're doing to yourself, to the world, to the fabric of the Universe! We rescue people like you and save the world at the same time!"

"Interesting." Tillie sat down on the couch and crossed her legs, leaning toward him slightly, one hand supporting her head, lips slightly parted, a pose calculated and perfected over the years to make men feel heard and to keep them talking. Her old career as an escort had prepared her perfectly for a new career in pretending to torture Auditors, apparently. "Tell me more."

And apparently, Auditors were no different from any other pathetic ego-driven man. The agent's chest puffed out with self-importance. He was about to start bragging.

"It's all about balance, you see. We have to keep the balance of the Universe, and balance is the reason why everyone has their own discipline. When people start dabbling outside of that, it throws everything out of whack."

"Mmm. You're so smart. I had no idea. Why do you suppose that is?"

He smirked. "That's okay. You've just never had the right guidance."

"Of course." She nodded emphatically. "I'm so glad you're here. Please tell me exactly what it is about dabbling outside my own discipline that throws off the balance of the Universe."

"Well, it's very complicated–" he began.

Great. In Tillie's experience, when a man backed out of mansplaining by claiming something was too complicated for her pretty little head, that meant he didn't actually know. Time to move on to a new topic.

"Oh, well, in that case, I probably shouldn't worry about it," she interjected. "Complicated things are just no fun at all."

The man beamed at her. She spared a moment of pride (and a little amusement) that she could sweet-talk any man, even when he was tied to a chair and hemmed in by spells.

"Tell me about you!" she said with a perky smile. "I want to know everything. Where do you live?"

"Oh, you know, here and there. Wherever the organization sends me."

"A traveling man! You must be very important. Do you get a lot of missions?"

He looked very pleased with himself. "I am very important. One of the best."

"I bet you are, a big strapping man like you. So, you don't have a permanent base? A headquarters where all the bigwigs hang out? Maybe an office where Auditors like yourself check in between missions?" Tillie leaned forward. "I'd love to be able to get in touch with you again."

"Well, I've only been called before the court a couple of times," he said, dismissively. "They don't do that much, actually, and they've become corrupt, lazy, and power-hungry. The real work is done out in the field. And there are the training facilities, of course, but I've been out of training for ages."

"The court? That sounds very interesting."

He shrugged. "If you like back-biting politicians and lazy-ass sycophants. There's really nothing much interesting about them at all. And they'll be irrelevant soon."

She sighed. More irrelevant people. Better steer the conversation back to why he was here.

"Well, even so, I'm so lucky that they sent you here. Why did they send you here, anyway?" Tillie leaned back casually, as though the question was just an afterthought. Nothing important. Just curious.

She knew instantly that it had been a mistake.

The man's face darkened and he seemed to wake up from the self-important daze she'd put him into. "They didn't send me. I—"

He broke off as the door opened and people began pouring in.

"You!" yelled Giovani. "What the hell are you up to?"

"I'm sorry, Tillie," called Scott. "I tried to stop them, but this guy just shoved past me."

Giovani whirled around. "Whose shields are these?"

"Mine," said Scott.

"Drop them," Giovani ordered.

Scott crossed his arms over his chest. "Now, wait just a moment. Who the hell are you? Those shields are all that's containing this guy. He broke in and attacked Tillie, you know."

Giovani stepped toward Scott. "Let me worry about containing Parker. Drop the shields."

Tillie stood up and stepped between the two. "If we could cease and desist with the testosterone-fueled power plays here?" She turned to Giovani. "I assume you know this man?"

He continued to glare at Scott, not replying.

Tillie turned to look at Mattie and Trevor, cocking her head in question.

"Yeah," said Mattie. "We ran into him at your funeral."

"That's a phrase I never thought I'd hear," Tillie muttered.

"He's an Auditor," put in Trevor.

"Yes, I had gathered that much," said Tillie. "How did he know I wasn't actually dead?"

"I don't think he did," said Trevor. "He was looking for Agent Miller. The one whose body we spelled to look like you."

A hiss filled the room and Tillie turned to look at the man tied to her mother's antique armchair. He clamped his lips together and the hissing stopped, but she had never seen a face so filled with despair.

Scott dropped his shields and Tillie watched as Trevor approached, crouching in front of the Auditor and placing his hands gently on the man's arms.

Agent Parker looked into Trevor's compassionate face. "She's dead?"

He nodded. "I'm sorry, but it was us or her. Who was she to you?"

The man shook his head, closing his eyes. "She was a visionary. A great woman who was going to change the world." His eyes snapped open again, this time filled with hate. The weight of his emotion battered at Tillie, but she gritted her teeth and remained in place.

Trevor, Mattie, and Giovani stood their ground as well, but Scott took a step back, and the Auditor fixed his eyes on the stocky speller. "You are all responsible for this. She would have changed everything. Brought the organization into the twenty-first century. We could have fixed the whole world. Brought balance to everything. The organization could have ruled the world."

"Oh, good," said Tillie. "Delusions of grandeur."

"And world domination," added Mattie, cheerfully.

Giovani stepped forward and touched Trevor's shoulder. "May I?"

Trevor nodded and stood up, allowing Giovani to take his place directly in front of Parker.

"You're saying Agent Miller was a renegade?" Giovani said, his voice steely. "Plotting to overthrow the order of the organization? How many of you are there?"

Agent Parker worked his mouth for a moment and then spit at Giovani.

Ignoring the spittle dripping down his cheek, Giovani crouched in front of Agent Parker. "I would also like to overthrow the organization."

"We're not planning to overthrow it, you abomination," said Agent Parker. "We don't want to take it down. We want to make it stronger. Modernize it. Do away with the court and put the power into the hands of the agents, where it belongs. Without the drain of the sycophants and the squabbling of the power-hungry court, the organization could be truly effective. We could wipe out the abominations once and for all and bring true balance to the world." By this point, the man was shouting and drool was running down his own chin.

Giovani narrowed his eyes. "And then what?"

"And then the world will be clean," Parker whispered.

Tillie strained to hear him.

"Clean and beautiful with everyone in their place."

Standing, Giovani finally wiped his face. "And I suppose you think your place would be toward the top."

Parker lifted his hate-filled eyes upward. "Agent Miller should have been at the top. She was everything. I would die for her in an instant. My place means nothing."

"Very well," said Giovani. "Then die." Before anyone could stop him, he moved his fingers in a stitch and Agent Parker slumped forward, all expression leaving his face.

Tillie watched as her sister rushed forward and touched the man's neck.

"He's dead," said Mattie, her face going ghost-white. She whirled toward Giovani. "What the hell did you do that for?"

Giovani's face was blank. "What else was there to do?"

"Well, for starters," said Mattie, "I would have liked to have asked him some questions myself."

"And for another," said Trevor, "hasn't anyone ever told you that murder is wrong?"

"Not recently," said Giovani, his lips twisting into a wry expression.

"Oh, dear."

Tillie turned toward the kitchen doorway and saw Ida Garaveldi holding a tray with one of her favorite tea sets. You could always count on Ida to make tea in any situation.

"Well, what's done is done, I always say," said Ida, briskly. She carried in the tea and began distributing the ceramic cups.

Tillie took hers and waited patiently as Ida poured for everyone, leaving Tillie for last. Tillie wrapped her hands around the cup and peered into its depths. She inhaled the earthy aroma of the green tea, holding it in her lungs and then exhaling with a deep sigh. Sipping the tea, she could feel herself relaxing, returning to the state she'd achieved by her yoga before all of the excitement.

"Thank you." She smiled at the elderly speller.

"Nothing in the world that tea can't fix, I always say," said Ida, smiling in return. "Well, except that." She nodded toward the dead man. "I guess tea isn't quite that miraculous. Still, no point in fretting about it."

Tillie nodded. "Yes, we had better start figuring out our next move."

"Do you think we could remove the corpse, first and foremost?" said Mattie. "I'm not super into the idea of chatting with a dead body around. To say nothing of the ick factor of a dead body just hanging out on Mom's favorite chair."

Tillie turned to Giovani. "I'm going to go out on a limb and say that you're probably the person here most acquainted with the process of hiding a body."

He shrugged. "Honestly, we never bothered."

"You just left a trail of bodies?" said Trevor. "How did you not get caught? Or is the prison system filled with Auditors?"

"Well, to be fair, we – they – Auditors don't kill people all that often," said Giovani. "The main goal is to take people alive and reprogram them. If that doesn't seem possible, then, yes, we'd kill them. And yes, we'd just leave them there. The fact is that law enforcement is most likely to assume literally anything except that the person was killed by agents of a shadowy secret society of mages."

"That's fair," said Tillie. "You probably also didn't kill them in someone else's living room."

"No," he admitted. "It was either in their own home or, if they'd managed to run, then in a motel or on the road somewhere."

"So there are probably people in prison out there who were convicted of murder done by an Auditor," said Mattie. "That's a real dick move."

Giovani threw up his hands. "I was brainwashed! Anyway, I've only killed three people."

"Including this guy?" asked Scott.

"Four people," said Giovani.

"That's not so bad," observed Ida. "I've killed more than that." She sipped at her tea. "Of course, those were in battle, not while they were tied to a chair. You get to be my age and you stick with magery, you'll rack up a body count, I suppose."

"Not me," said Scott. "I'm a pacifist."

"Well," said Tillie. "War happens, though, doesn't it?"

"Can't stop it," said Ida. "All you can do is make sure you stay on the side that's standing for goodness, I always say."

"How did you kill him anyway?" asked Trevor. He walked over to the corpse, walking around it and examining it.

"I stitched his heart still," said Giovani.

Tillie stared at him. "Stitchers can stop a heart?"

"Not exactly," he said.

Ida snapped her fingers. "You combined a stitch and a spell!" she said. "That's very clever, I suppose, but also very scary. I'm glad you're on our side, Giovani."

"You are on our side, aren't you?" said Tillie.

"Of course I'm on your side," said Giovani, his voice full of wary weariness. "I just killed a man for you."

"Nobody asked you to do that," muttered Mattie.

Scott cleared his throat. "You know, I could use some backstory. Until I heard her yelling, I thought Tillie was dead. I only just learned the other day that Auditors are actually real, and I didn't quite believe it until this guy broke in. I don't know who you are." He nodded at Giovani and then at Ida. "I know you, ma'am, but only by reputation. And I have no idea what the Auditors are really about or why this guy broke in here, especially if he thought Tillie was actually dead, and I sure as hell don't know what I'm doing mixed up in it all, or if I'd prefer to just go home and forget I ever saw you."

"Pacifist or not," said Ida, "you're here now, and you'd better make an informed decision about whether you'd like to get involved or leave us to our battles."

"Then inform me, please."

"Fair enough," murmured Tillie. She set her tea down on an end table and approached the dead Auditor. "Let's get this into the ritual room for now, and then we can enjoy our tea and get Scott up to speed."

Carefully, she reached out and untied one arm. Out of the corner of her eye, she saw Mattie picking at the other.

"Hey," said Mattie. "Is this my yarn?"

"Yes, sorry," said Tillie. "It was all I saw on hand."

"You know this is angora." Mattie tugged at a strand of yarn. "This shit is not cheap."

"Well, excuse me for prioritizing my own life," Tillie snapped. "I'll pay you back for it."

"No, no," Mattie muttered. "When you put it that way, I'd be petty to expect that."

The yarn twitched out of Tillie's hands and she jumped back in startlement.

"If you two are done squabbling?" said Trevor, lowering his hands, which were now full of yarn. He must have stitched it free. Tillie was going to have to get used to her best friend using mage powers.

Tillie nodded her head. "Sorry."

"Me too," muttered Mattie.

"I feel like I'm back in high school," said Trevor. "I'm not going to be your buffer now, so you better learn to co-exist, especially if we're going to keep up the illusion that Tillie is dead and Mattie is living here by herself."

He moved his fingers again in an elaborate gesture and they glowed. The body of the Auditor disappeared from the chair, hopefully onto the floor in the ritual room and not onto one of Tillie's lovely suede fainting couches.

"I could get used to having a stitcher around." Tillie grinned at Trevor and he grinned back.

"Don't abuse our friendship," he admonished.

"Better yet," said Giovani. "Learn how to stitch for yourself. Learn how to use each discipline and then how to combine them like I have."

"That's impossible," said Scott.

"Yes," agreed Giovani. "We've all been told that it's impossible. Turns out it isn't, though."

"Start at the beginning," ordered Ida from her seat on the couch. "That's the best way to tell a story, I always say." Her voice took on a steely quality that showed Tillie why Ida had a reputation for being the most formidable speller in St. Louis, a reputation that had always seemed at odds with Trevor's sweet, scatterbrained neighbor. "Start fifteen years ago, when you started getting too big for your britches. Tell us what happened to you before and after your father and I rushed into your living room and saw you taken by the Auditors. Tell us your story, Giovani Garaveldi, and be honest because I know you, young man. And I will not forgive any lapses, any posturing, anything tweaked to make yourself look better. You tell us your truth."

"Yes, Auntie," said Giovani. He took a deep breath.

Tillie studied his face. This was not the confident mystery man who had warned her of the Auditors coming. Nor did she recognize the brutal efficiency of the man who had barged into her condo just a few minutes before and ruthlessly executed a member of his own former society. This was a nephew chastised by his aunt.

She sat down beside Ida, picked up her tea, and took another blissful sip, settling in for the long story. Her cat, Max, jumped up beside her and she stroked his ears.

"You all know the beginning of my story," Giovani began.

"I don't," interrupted Scott.

"Tell him the whole thing," ordered Ida. She leaned forward and smiled at Scott. "I don't think we've been introduced, young man."

"I know who you are, Miss Garaveldi," he said, somewhat nervously.

She waved her hands at him gently. "No, no. You call me Ida."

"Oh." He looked startled and somehow even more nervous. "Okay. And I'm Scott."

Ida nodded emphatically. "Scott. Very nice to meet you. You look familiar. Who are your people?"

"I'm a Holmes. My mom's family aren't mages, but my dad's are," he said.

"Holmes, Holmes," Ida tapped her fingers against her lips for a moment and then brightened. "Why, I went to school with Sandy Holmes! Lovely girl. Very nice. Stitcher, I think she was."

"Yes, that's right," said Scott. "My great-aunt."

"Excellent. And you're a speller, I suppose, dear?"

He nodded.

"Wonderful!" Ida beamed at Scott. Then she turned back to Giovani and scowled. "Now I won't ask you again, young man. Start at the beginning."

"Yes, Auntie." Giovani nodded humbly.

Tillie met Trevor's dancing eyes across the room and found her lips twitching. She took another sip of tea to hide her amusement. At least they knew that if Giovani got "too big for his britches" again, Ida could keep him in line.

"I was a very cocky child," Giovani began.

Ida nodded approvingly.

"And I got worse as I got older. I was always a very powerful seer, but in my teen years, I started getting bored with it. I started wondering why, if I was so powerful, I couldn't do spells and stitches too. So I started trying.

"I failed for a long time. To be honest, I think it was because I was so cocky – I was so arrogant that I just assumed that I would be able to pick up the other disciplines as quickly as I'd picked up seeing when I was a kid. So when it didn't happen like that, I worked less hard at it instead of redoubling my efforts as I should have."

"So, why did the Auditors target you, then?" asked Trevor.

Giovani smiled ruefully. "Sometimes all you need is some external motivation. I had a few beers with some friends one night a couple of years later and I started bragging about how I'd managed to do a small spell once. They didn't believe me. I tried again to do the spell, but of course, I was drunk and hadn't been practicing, so I completely failed. One of my other friends, also a seer, tried the same spell and succeeded, just for a moment. And in that moment, among the jeers of my friends, I resolved to show them all. I would learn how to spell. And stitch."

Tillie rolled her eyes. "So they triple-dog-dared you, and you couldn't resist. Typical machismo."

"Yes," he agreed. "So lies the folly of men."

"Only completely idiotic men," Trevor muttered.

"And you followed through?" Mattie raised her eyebrows.

Giovani nodded. "The very next day. I woke up with a massive hangover, popped some ibuprofen and ate a slinger, and got to work. It took me months to get to the point where I felt capable enough to start bragging again. But brag I did. What I wasn't expecting was that my friends would be unimpressed. They assumed it was parlor tricks. That I had someone hiding nearby making my hands glow, making the things move. I pointed out that my other friend had managed it, and they laughed and said they were drunk that night, they probably imagined it or it was a fluke."

He paused, his face darkening as he remembered. "I was so angry. My anger just pushed me to try harder, perfect my techniques. I got to the point where I could spell without saying any words aloud, without even my lips moving. I was as good at spelling as some natural spellers. I started learning to stitch too. That came more slowly. I believe that the farther a skill is from your natural discipline, the harder it is to learn. This is where spellers have an advantage, since stitching and seeing would be equidistant."

Tillie frowned. "If you were so vocal about it, how come it took so long for you to get caught? I was only teaching myself to spell for a couple of months, and I only told a couple of people about it, and they came after me right away."

Giovani shrugged. "Probably a combination of factors. The organization was under new leadership when I was brought in. The Pontiff is more established now–"

"The Pontiff?" interrupted Trevor. "Isn't that the Pope?"

"That's what we call the leader of the organization," said Giovani. "Maybe it comes from our medieval roots. A lot of the internal vocabulary is sort of churchy."

"Anyway, it's possible that things move more slowly during a power shift. Or that the former Pontiff wasn't as ruthless as the current one. It's also possible that my last name protected me to a certain extent."

"Why?" said Mattie.

"The Garaveldis are basically mage royalty, at least here in the Midwest," said Tillie. "They're an old family that produces really powerful mages, generation after generation."

"Well," said Ida. "I don't know about 'royalty.' We're well-thought-of, I suppose. But it seems a bit extreme to say that we're royalty."

Tillie couldn't help but notice that Ida looked very pleased, despite her words. She grinned. "You're a queen and you know it, Ida."

"A dowager, I suppose, at this time of my life," she demurred.

"I said 'queen,' and I meant it. Are you calling me a liar?" Tillie raised an eyebrow.

Ida smiled broadly. "Well, I've never known you to flatter, so I suppose I'd better take you at your word. Never accuse someone of something outside of their character, I always say."

"Whatever the reason," Giovani continued, "it took them nearly a year to come after me. And I managed to fight them off a couple of times. I should have run. Or told someone about them. My dad, maybe, or you, Auntie. Especially since you'd been warning me ever since I'd started."

"Wait, you knew about the Auditors?" said Scott to Ida.

"I didn't know that it was the Auditors, per se," she replied. "All I knew was that my own aunt, Ines, and her fiancé, Christopher, had disappeared years earlier after they'd been learning magic outside their disciplines. I was worried the same thing would happen to Giovani."

"And I should have listened," he said.

"You regret learning to spell and stitch?" said Trevor. He was studying Giovani's face closely.

Tillie sat up a little straighter. She'd learned through the years to trust Trevor's instincts. What was he getting at?

Giovani paused thoughtfully. "No, I don't. Not anymore."

"You regret getting caught," said Mattie.

"Yes. If I had listened to Auntie Ida, I could have continued to learn, but done it more secretively so they wouldn't have known. Or evaded them more easily when they found me. Or fought back for longer and more effectively."

"They would have brought you in eventually, though, right?" said Tillie. She shivered. "They seemed pretty relentless when they were chasing me down."

"Oh, absolutely," said Giovani. "They don't give up on anyone. You did the right thing, faking your death. If you'd just killed the agents, that would have given you some time, but not much. Standard procedure is to check in with your handler each night. If a team doesn't check in three nights in a row, they're presumed dead and the handler will comb the news to see if they took the target down with them. If there's no mention of the target being dead, they'll send a new team."

"What about the agents?" asked Mattie.

Giovani looked at her for a moment as though waiting for more. Finally, he prompted, "What about them?"

"What's the procedure for coming after your presumed-dead agents?"

He shrugged. "There is none. If they're alive, they'll come back in and be reassigned. If they're not, they won't." He paused again. "Remember that most of these agents will have already been presumed dead by the outside world. Once we're taken to be re-educated, we have no contact with our families, our friends, anyone from our previous life. Tillie's 'body' was easily identified in the fire because the shop owner told them who she was and they matched it with the missing person report filed by Trevor here in St. Louis. No one was there to tell them who Agent Stone was, so he was most likely reported as a John Doe, and if he had never been arrested or anything, his identifying characteristics, such as they are after a fire, probably weren't in any kind of database. And, while there probably was a missing person report for him at some point, it's most likely been closed by now."

"So his family and Agent Miller's will never know what happened to them," said Mattie, softly. Her eyes met Tillie's across the room. "That would have been you."

"If you hadn't come after me," Tillie reminded her. She stood and strode toward her sister, reaching out an arm to snag Trevor along the way, and folded them both into a group hug.

Giovani cleared his throat. "I think I had a little to do with your continued existence in this world as well."

"We'd have found her," said Trevor, determination in his voice. "Even if the Auditors had taken Tillie, we'd have rescued her."

"No," Giovani said, soberly. "You wouldn't have. Let me tell you a little bit about what happened after they finally got me."

Tillie tried to re-settle herself near Mattie, but there wasn't a comfortable seat, and besides, her tea was still over by the couch and Max was giving her a betrayed look for abandoning him. She crossed back over and sat down again, returning her full attention to Giovani and his story. Her cat crawled onto her lap to prevent her from getting up again.

"First of all, they take you to a new city, chosen at random, so that even if someone is looking for you, they won't be looking in the right spot. Plus, even if you manage to escape, you'll be lost and disoriented in an unfamiliar locale. They're not idiots. They've been doing this for literally centuries, and they know damn well that they're dealing with powerful mages - no one who isn't powerful tries to dabble outside their scope – who have unpredictable abilities.

"Usually, they manage to catch mages before they get to the point where they're actually proficient in their newfound skills, but they never assume that. There have been mages who weren't found out until they'd been practicing for years. Honestly, those mages usually end up dead rather than taken. If a team of agents can't bring someone in, we're taught to switch to kill-mode pretty early on. Those mages don't take so well to the re-education anyway.

"Secondly, the training facilities are insanely secure. Because, again, these standards have been honed over a very, very long time. The Auditors have been around, in one form or another, since the sixth century."

Trevor nodded. "Right. La Société des Arbitres Mystiques."

Giovani stared at him. "La what?"

"That was the original name of the organization," said Trevor. "You didn't know that?"

"I guess they didn't think it was worth mentioning in the history lessons," said Giovani. "Just that we'd – they'd – been around for centuries, first out in the open, and then underground and that we've always been the only ones standing between the world and the evils of power-grabbing mages who want to expand their range, at the cost of the very fabric of the Universe."

"So dramatic," Tillie murmured.

"Are we sure that's not correct, though?" said Scott.

"Whose side are you on?" demanded Mattie.

"Not the side of the crazy secret society nut-cases," he retorted. "But it seems like it could be a little more nuanced, right?"

"It could," conceded Giovani. "But I think not. I think this is a case of a group of people who were once very politically powerful and are still very wealthy, who want to remain so. And of course, the organization is run by the court, who is still very politically powerful within the organization and, again, wants to keep it that way. The official line is that the organization went underground because the mage community as a whole had been purged and only a smaller presence was needed. They tell us that it was thought by the leaders at the time that a clandestine organization would be more effective at ferreting out those few mages who needed to be stopped. I have recently come to believe that the actual thinking was that a clandestine organization would be easier for the court to control, as they found their political pull in the greater outside world waning."

"You're saying they deliberately created for themselves a smaller pond to be big fish in?" said Trevor. "That's interesting."

"But what makes you think that learning new disciplines is okay?" persisted Scott. "How do we know that's not just what you want to think because you want to keep doing it? And if you've been re-educated by these guys, what are you even doing here? Why aren't you out there, being a good little agent still?"

"No, no," said Ida. "No skipping ahead to the end. I'd like an answer to the first question, but we'll need to hear about the whole shebang before you get to why you left. It's hard enough to follow a story like this without skipping around."

"If it's okay with you, auntie, I'd like to hold off on answering the first question too," said Giovani.

"And why is that?"

"Because it's connected to the rest. I'm no longer a good little agent because of what I found out. That makes me think the court and the Pontiff are full of shit." Giovani paused uncertainly. He took a deep breath and let it out. "It was something my son said."

Ida, who was always a straight-spined woman, somehow managed to sit even more upright. "Your what?"

Giovani winced. "See, I didn't want to do that quite yet."

Ida jumped to her feet, her eyes blazing and her hands glowing.

Just in time, Tillie cried out a Latin word and threw a shield up between the two Garaveldi mages. She stood, spilling Max down onto the floor, and then staggered as the brunt of the magical attack struck her shield and she felt it weaken.

"A little help here," she called to the other mages in the room.

Mattie and Scott leaped into action.

Scott built a second, stronger shield in front of Tillie's and she dropped hers. Mattie had already grabbed her hand, so she took Scott's and funneled mage energy into him. Trevor put a hand on Scott's arm, presumably also lending him strength.

Ida's magical onslaught continued, tossing bolts of pure destructive energy toward her nephew as she ranted. "We do not do things this way in our family, young man. You kept your son from us? From your father? What kind of place is a secret society to raise a child? Who knows what kind of nonsense they've filled his head with? He is a Garaveldi!"

Giovani stood, head bowed, as though simply waiting for the shield to fail and his inevitable death.

"Say something, Giovani!" snapped Mattie. "We can't hold this up forever! Ida is too strong!"

He lifted his head. "No. She's right. I fucked up. There is no redemption for me."

Trevor intervened. "No redemption? You were brainwashed. Do you know what kind of trauma that creates? You had literally no option but to follow along with what your captors told you. The fact that you escaped without outside intervention – that's incredibly impressive."

"And you can redeem yourself by helping me and other targets of the Auditors," added Tillie. "And by getting your son out of the clutches of the Auditors and into the loving embrace of your family."

Ida finally paused, lowering her hands. "He belongs with us."

Tillie caught Trevor's eye and jerked her head toward Ida.

Trevor nodded slightly and stepped toward his neighbor, touching her shoulder.

Ida looked up at him, face still furious. Her hands had stopped glowing, however, and Tillie found herself relaxing slightly.

"We need to rescue this kid," said Trevor, gently. "And we can't do that if you kill his father."

Ida nodded. "I'd probably regret that, wouldn't I?"

Tillie relaxed further.

Taking her seat again, Ida picked up her teacup and took a sip. "I hope you can forgive me, Giovani. I reacted without thinking."

Giovani took a deep breath in. "I am the one who begs your forgiveness, auntie," he said carefully. "And rescuing Marco is a priority of mine, but I needed to get myself free before I could do that. He's very well taken care of."

"Marco." Ida smiled. "A good name. How old is Marco?"

"Eight," said Giovani.

"Is he a seer?" asked Ida.

"A stitcher," said Giovani. "And a powerful one."

"We will get him out," said Mattie. "And take the whole fucking organization down."

Giovani shook his head. "How do you suggest we take down a centuries-old secret society full of the most powerful and fanatical mages in the world? Their agents are spread out across the globe, and if you kill one pair, which we've already done, more will just take their place." He gestured toward the chair Agent Parker had been tied to. "Which has also already happened."

"Well, you know what they say about vipers," said Trevor.

"Avoid them?" said Mattie.

"No, I mean, like, about their heads," he clarified.

"Step on them!" said Scott.

"No!" Trevor sighed. "You know…. How do you kill a viper?"

"Oh, right," said Mattie. "Cut off its head."

"So." He quirked an eyebrow. "What is the viper's head?"

Giovani frowned. "I see where you're going with this, but killing the Pontiff won't fix anything. They'll just appoint a new one."

"From the court, right?" said Tillie.

Mattie jumped to her feet. "So we take out the whole damn court!"

Tillie studied Giovani's face. "Would that work?"

He shook his head. "We'd have to find them – they rove around, moving every six months or so. We'd have to find out where they are right now, then somehow take them off-guard, and then somehow make sure we take them all out at once, without giving anyone a chance to take charge."

"And if we did that?" she persisted. "Would that work?"

Giovani's eyes met hers and he smiled slightly. "Yeah. I think that'd work."

3.

The next morning, Tillie rolled out of bed with a smile. No more lolling about in some kind of undead – or at least fake dead – limbo! She had a purpose in life again! Time to dismantle an evil society of power-hungry bastards!

She pulled off the silky negligee she had slept in and replaced it with a sports bra and a pair of yoga pants.

Grabbing the bottle of water she kept by her bed, she strode to the empty space in the middle of her bedroom and rolled out a mat to begin her morning workout, starting with stretches then moving into some krav maga moves.

Tillie had started taking krav maga as a workout, but it had definitely come in handy over the past few weeks of fighting, so she wanted to make sure she kept it up, even if she wasn't able to go to the studio and practice sparring with her class.

She was primarily a seer, which wasn't ideal for combat situations, but when combined with a martial art, it had proven pretty handy. Seeing gave her an unparalleled defense and the krav maga rounded out the offense.

Tillie made a mental note to talk to Giovani about how to combine seeing and spelling, which seemed like it would be even more useful in mage combat.

Then again, it seemed to take some mages off-guard when their magical attack was met with a physical one.

She smiled as she executed a particularly tricky kick-punch-kick combination. She was starting to sweat and she pushed herself into a higher gear, moving as quickly as she could, imagining Agent Miller in front of her again.

Finally, feeling good, she began to slow her movements, ending the workout with more stretching. She sank into a lotus and ran through some deep breathing exercises.

When she was done, Tillie stood up, smiling to herself as she rolled up her mat once more. She chugged the rest of her water and sauntered into the kitchen to make a smoothie.

Mattie was already there, seated at the breakfast bar, finishing off the rest of last night's pizza. After deciding that they were going to take down the Auditors, the group had been a little too excitable for making any real plans. They had agreed to head their separate ways and meet up the next morning.

Then Mattie and Trevor had insisted on ordering pizza before he went home. Apparently, all there had been to eat at the funeral had been cheese.

"Good morning," said her sister, cheerfully. "How come you're all sweaty?"

"I just finished working out." Tillie frowned. "Is pizza really the first choice you want to make in the morning?"

"Yep – I like to start my days happy," said Mattie. "Exercising seems like a terrible way to start out."

"When do you usually work out?" Tillie asked.

"I don't," said Mattie.

Tillie raised an eyebrow. "You look just as good as me. How is that possible?"

"Thank you?" said Mattie. "Yeah, I'm gonna go ahead and take that as a compliment. I guess it must suck to find out that you didn't actually have to do all that exercising, huh?"

Tillie rolled her eyes. "I think if you tried it, you'd find more benefits than just a rocking body. That is how I start my day happy." She opened the freezer drawer and pulled out a bag of mixed berries, setting them on the counter and then hitting up the fridge for some yogurt and pomegranate juice.

"I guess I do like to keep a pretty active life – just nothing so formal as a work-out. I'll need to find some good hiking around here," said Mattie. "And I don't suppose you have a bike I could borrow? I remember taking the bus in St. Louis back in the day, and I'm not looking forward to it, but I can't really afford to buy a new car."

"It's improved a lot, actually, since they put in the Metrolink – the light rail," said Tillie absently, as she assembled her smoothie. "Are you sure you wouldn't rather have something healthy for breakfast? There's plenty of berries."

"Nah, I'm good." Mattie popped the last of the pizza crust into her mouth and stood up. "So, that's a no on the bike?"

"No, I have one. I don't think I've ever used it," Tillie said. "It's down in my storage locker in the basement. Trevor and I were thinking about taking up biking at some point, but we decided on krav maga instead. To be honest, I'm glad we did."

"Well, I'm glad you considered the biking enough to buy me one," said Mattie. "In that case, I'm going to go to the grocery store this morning. I'm tired of all your healthy food."

"Fine, just keep the junk food out of sight, please. All those garish labels would really mess up my vibe in here." Tillie poured the smoothie into a glass and inserted a silicon-tipped stainless steel straw. She took a sip, savoring it on her tongue before swallowing. So tart and delicious. "You're really missing out here," she told her sister.

"I disagree," Mattie laughed. "Can we grab that bike now?"

"Oh, sure." Tillie ran a hand through her short, damp hair and snagged a sapphire cardigan from the back of a chair. She pulled it on and led the way out into the hall, pausing to grab her keys off their hook beside the door.

"What time are we all getting back together today for our scheming?" asked Mattie as they descended the cool marble stairs.

"Eleven, I think," said Tillie, absently. "You should have plenty of time to run to the store and back. Field Foods is closest, but if you want junk food, you'll probably need to go to Schnuck's."

"I need junk food," said Mattie. "It's really an addiction at this point."

Tillie opened her mouth to respond but snapped it shut when a familiar feeling tugged at her eyes. Something was about to happen. She switched her sight into seer mode and immediately grabbed Mattie and pulled her down.

Mattie sat down beside her and looked around. After a moment, she whispered, "What's going on?"

Tillie put a finger to her lips. Three, two, one.

And a dart whistled over their heads.

Seizing Mattie's hand, Tillie pulled her back up and the pair dashed back the way they'd come, rounding the corner of the stairwell just in time to see the door to the second floor slamming shut.

Mattie reached for the door handle, but Tillie stopped her, shaking her head. She flattened herself against the wall and Mattie followed suit. Another moment and the door opened once again.

Tillie was already reaching for the arm of their assailant, swinging her around to face them.

Mattie was only a step behind her, and as Tillie dragged the woman into the stairwell, Mattie's hands glowed and their attacker froze, stiff and motionless.

"Nice trick," said Tillie, switching back into normal sight mode.

"Thanks," said Mattie. "Of course, now we can't ask her any questions."

"Well, we can ask," said Tillie. "But I guess she can't answer."

"Probably can't use your feminine wiles on her either, like you did the last one," said Mattie.

"My wiles are pretty powerful," said Tillie. "You'd be surprised who they work on."

"Fair enough," said Mattie. "Let's just get her up to your place."

"Yes. I've been working on something, actually, that might help." Tillie inhaled deeply and concentrated on her spell. When she was sure she had the right headspace, she spoke a Latin word, and the frozen woman levitated off the ground.

"Nice one!" said Mattie. "You know it doesn't have to be Latin, though, right?"

Tillie nodded but didn't respond, instead repeating the word over and over again under her breath. She couldn't actually hold a tricky spell like that without constant reinforcement.

Mattie cocked her head and narrowed her eyes. "What are you doing?"

Exasperated, Tillie simply gestured to her sister to guide the woman back up the stairs.

"Okay." Mattie still looked confused, but grabbed their attacker and pushed her toward Tillie's condo.

When they finally reached the door, Tillie opened it, still chanting softly, and led the way to the couch. She grabbed the woman's arm and positioned her above the sofa, and then finally stopped the words.

A second later, the levitation spell dissipated and the woman crashed downward. Tillie winced and reached forward, moving their captive's limbs like a doll's to position her in a more comfortable pose.

She turned toward Mattie. "I'm not a natural speller. I have to keep repeating a spell or I can't maintain it. And it's easier for me to use a more formal word, like Latin, to think of a spell as something anyone can use, rather than something I just made up."

Mattie frowned. "But Giovani keeps spells going without all of that. He's a natural seer."

Tillie shrugged. "Maybe I'll be able to do it more easily with practice. Have you tried seeing or stitching?"

"No," Mattie admitted. "I figured I still need to get spelling down before I can branch out."

"You'll probably have similar issues, then," said Tillie. "It will be really interesting, actually, to see what the pitfalls are for you. I wonder how someone who isn't a natural seer will be able to even activate the sight. I mean, when I do it–"

"Yeah, that's really interesting," Mattie interrupted. "But maybe we could focus right now on this lady who just tried to kill us?"

"Oh, right." Tillie turned her focus back to the present moment. "Can you keep her body frozen but unfreeze her face so she can talk to us?"

"I think so." Mattie turned to face the couch and the glow around her hands pulsed briefly.

"Abominations!" shrieked the woman.

Great. This again. "I am getting really tired of being called that," said Tillie. "I mean, I've been called a lot of things in the course of my career. I'm used to people being dismissive or judgemental of sex workers, calling us whores, sluts, etcetera. Abomination is one that even the Evangelicals have never used. And now, suddenly, it's like I can't go one day without the word being hurled at me."

"Zero points for creativity," agreed Mattie. "At least this confirms that she's an Auditor."

"What else would she be?" said Tillie.

"I don't know," said Mattie, thoughtfully. "Giovani keeps saying that the Auditors shouldn't be coming after us, so every time I see one, I think maybe it's someone else. A little variety would be nice."

"You're right," said Tillie. She turned to the Auditor. "Why do you keep coming after us? We have it on good authority that you shouldn't be bothering because I'm officially dead."

"I don't have to tell you anything," the woman spat. "You're nothing but an abomination."

Tillie sighed. "Yes, I know."

"Are you Agent Parker's partner?" asked Mattie.

The woman looked wary. "What do you know about Agent Parker?"

"We know he's de —"

"He was here yesterday!" Tillie interrupted. What was Mattie thinking, giving away important details? Spellers. Just rushing into everything.

Tillie grabbed Mattie's arm. "Can I see you in the kitchen for a moment?" she hissed.

She strode into the other room and then spun around, smacking Mattie on the arm. "What do you think you're doing?"

"I have no idea," said Mattie. "This is my first interrogation."

"Well, generally it's a good idea to get information from your captive, not give them info they don't need and which might make them less likely to talk," said Tillie.

"Right. That makes sense." Mattie sighed. "I guess we need a plan. I suck at plans."

Tillie smiled ruefully. "I know. Luckily, I'm fantastic at them."

Mattie grinned. "It's nice to have you on my team, sis."

Tapping a finger on her lips, Tillie thought for a moment. "Let's do a good-cop/bad-cop thing, shall we? Maybe you go in and offer her a drink or a snack, tell her that we just want to talk, we're not going to hurt her, we're all mages in this together, and so on."

"How would she eat or drink if she's frozen? I don't think feeding her like a parakeet would bolster her dignity much."

"Okay, well, just go in and be nice. Maybe make her more comfortable in some way."

"I could do that. And then you come in and just slap her across the face?"

"I was thinking something a little more subtle." Tillie switched into seer mode and ran through a few scenarios. "Yes, I think this will do nicely. Instead of good-cop/bad-cop, we'll do good-mage/abomination." She returned her eyes to their typical blue and quickly outlined a plan for Mattie.

"Sounds good!" Mattie squared her shoulders and marched out into the other room.

Tillie had to admit that was one advantage of working with a speller as opposed to a seer or stitcher. A speller would act without hesitation.

Seers, herself included, tended to make a lot of plans and then waffle over which was best. In the past, she had often forced herself to take action by asking what Mattie would do.

And then there were stitchers, who just got bogged down in examining every detail of what had come before, and never quite seemed to get to what to do next.

She and Trevor balanced each other out nicely. Actually, Trevor would be useful in this situation. He wasn't supposed to come over for another hour.

Tillie grabbed her phone from its charger on the counter and sent him a quick text, urging him to come over sooner and outlining a part he could play. She glanced at the time again. Mattie was probably just about ready for her.

She dropped the phone into the pocket on the side of her cardigan and buttoned it up.

Then she schooled her face into an appropriate scowl and stalked into the doorway, stopping short, as though finding something unexpected.

"What the hell are you doing?" she yelled at Mattie, who was busily arranging the frozen mage's legs on the couch, propping them comfortably up on a cushion. "Need I remind you that she attacked us?"

"Hey, now," said Mattie. "I don't think there's any call for that. You mishandled things badly enough yesterday. I'm taking control now."

"She is the enemy!" Tillie hissed. "And I don't give a flying fuck what you think, I'm glad I killed that bastard!"

The captive Auditor's eyes widened and Tillie suppressed a smile. So the woman *was* here for Agent Parker.

"Well, you're not killing this one," Mattie retorted. "And you know what? I think she might have a point. You *are* an abomination."

The Auditor smirked.

Tillie glared at her. "You think this is funny? We'll see how funny you think it is when my spells flay you alive."

"You can barely spell at all," the woman retorted. "You're kidding yourself if you think you're good for anything but your little eye tricks."

She closed the distance between them and leaned down until her face was inches away from the captive's, deliberately pushing Mattie aside and putting some space between them. "My little eye tricks saw you coming. My spell allowed us to get you up here. And yesterday I used stitching and spelling together to peel the flesh from your little friend's bones."

"Tillie!" said Mattie. "That's enough! Get away from her!"

Spinning around, Tillie rushed toward her sister.

The glow around Mattie's hands brightened, and Tillie found herself frozen. It was . . . very unpleasant. No wonder that Auditor was cranky.

She could still breathe and she could see and hear and presumably her heart was still beating. But her muscles were already starting to ache from her instinctive efforts to move them. Hmm. She wondered if anyone had ever considered opening a mage gym using this spell for resistance-training.

Tillie wrestled her attention back to her sister's voice, which was talking to the Auditor again.

" — sick of the way she is constantly trying to be more than she should be. Why can't she be content with being a seer?"

"She is an abomination," agreed the Auditor.

"Yes. You know, maybe you should get yourself a thesaurus," said Mattie. "She's an abomination, sure, but she is also an atrocity. An outrage. A disgrace."

Tillie tried to roll her eyes, but they wouldn't roll. This really sucked. She was also concerned about the lack of ability to blink. What would happen to her sight, magical and otherwise, if her eyes dried out?

"An abomination," repeated the Auditor, but her voice seemed less sure.

"What's your name?" asked Mattie.

"Shezza," said the Auditor. "Agent Shezza."

"What's your first name?" said Mattie. "I'm Mattie. The abomination over there is Tillie."

"You will call me Agent Shezza."

"Oh, fine," said Mattie. "Then you have to call me Ms. Holiday."

"I will call you abomination."

"Hey! I'm not an abomination! All I do is spells," Mattie protested.

"You've been sheltering her," said Agent Shezza. "Helping her escape her Audit. We can help her change. She could become like me and save the world, instead of destroying it."

Huh. Tillie hadn't really considered the fact that every agent was once what they considered an abomination. Damn – now they had her using the word too. She wondered idly how they could use that in their favor. Trevor had probably already started researching deconditioning techniques.

Her phone chirped and she automatically tried to reach toward it. A stabbing pain struck her arm muscles. Hopefully, that was Trevor confirming that he'd be here soon.

Tillie tried to sigh, but she couldn't even do that.

Mattie was talking again. "Say I was interested in joining up. How would I do that?"

Agent Shezza didn't respond. Tillie wished she had been frozen facing the action. Why wasn't she saying anything?

"Do you have a website or something?" Mattie prompted.

"No one joins up," said Agent Shezza, slowly. "I guess you could. But no one ever does."

Great. This woman was an idiot.

Mattie changed tacks. "Well, maybe you could come back tomorrow with a pamphlet. Don't you guys work in teams? Where's your partner?"

"My partner was Agent Parker." There was venom in Agent Shezza's voice.

"And you came here looking for him," said Mattie. "But why was he here? Did you know that Tillie was still alive?"

"He was looking for Agent Miller." There was something new in her voice. Respect? No, adulation. This woman had looked up to Agent Miller, adored her.

"Who is Agent Miller?"

Agent Shezza's voice spiraled upward again. "You will not speak of her! Abomination!"

Tillie longed for the ability to close her aching eyelids.

"Again, though," said Mattie. "I'm not an abomination. She's the abomination. Maybe it'll help if I unfreeze your arms."

Yes, please! Oh, wait, she was talking to the enemy, not her loving sister. Tillie reminded herself that this was her own plan. It didn't help much.

"There. Is that better? Would you like something to eat? We have cookies. Or maybe some water. Would you like something else? Tea? Coffee? A beer, maybe?"

"I will not eat your cookies, abomination."

This bitch was such a drama queen.

"No problem," said Mattie. Her voice sounded forcedly cheerful. "So, let's talk some more about Agent Parker. Did he tell you he was coming here?"

"Yes. He went to the abomination's funeral and found the rogue abomination there."

"The rogue— You mean Giovani?"

"Agent Garaveldi."

"Right. So, then he decided to come here?"

"He was suspicious. Agent Miller wouldn't have abandoned us. The rogue abomination must have kidnapped her."

"It didn't occur to you that she might be dead?" said Mattie.

Tillie held her breath. If the Auditor knew or suspected her hero was truly dead, she might stop talking, or worse, attack them again. She reminded herself that the Auditor was a stitcher, so as long as her hands were frozen, she wouldn't be able to attack.

"Agent Miller would not abandon us," repeated Agent Shezza.

"Fair enough," said Mattie. "So he came here?"

"He knew you were living here. He thought to check for clues. Then he failed to return to base."

"Why didn't you come with him?"

Agent Shezza sounded regretful. "I disagreed with him. I wanted to wait longer for Agent Miller. Not rock the boat."

"Does the organization know you're here?"

Silence.

Tillie longed to be able to see. What was going on?

"I'm going to take that as a no," said Mattie. "So, here's what I don't get, though. You're clearly very dedicated to the Auditors' cause. Hunting down abominations and whatever. Right?"

"Of course."

"But you also seem to be rebelling against them. Why?"

"The court has deviated from the cause."

"Interesting. Could you elaborate on that, please?"

"Why would I do that?"

Tillie noticed that whenever Mattie stuck to very simple, direct questions, Agent Shezza answered them almost automatically. When she got clever with her interrogation, asking anything that required thought or could be interpreted in different ways, Shezza seemed to realize that she shouldn't be talking to her. This must be related to her conditioning.

Of course, there was no way for Tillie to tell Mattie that. Maybe freezing her had been the wrong way to handle things.

"What is the court doing that you disagree with?"

"They are filled with corruption. All they care about is jockeying for power. The power should be in the hands of the agents. We are the ones who are doing the work. We are the true Auditors."

Ah. So, this was about power. Wasn't everything? Tillie's lips fought to curve into a smile. Her face throbbed in pain. She really, really hoped Trevor was about to walk in that door any moment and demand that Mattie release her from the spell.

And just then, on cue, she heard the door open and Trevor's voice – that beautiful, familiar, deep voice – shout, "What the hell is going on here?"

"Abomination!" shouted Agent Shezza.

Apparently, in her mind, everyone was an abomination until proven innabominative. Or was it unabominative? Nonabominative? Mattie would know.

"We have another visitor," said Mattie. "She's got some interesting things to say."

"What has she done to Tillie?" he demanded. "Release her at once!"

"Yes, please release her," said Mattie.

"What? But—"

"I said let her go!" Mattie interrupted.

"I'm not even—"

There was a slapping sound.

"What are you—"

This was going to be tricky if the Auditor couldn't play along. This was the part where Mattie was supposed to be convincing Agent Shezza that she was on her side and willing to play double agent. But if she was too stupid to figure out that Mattie was playing Trevor, it wouldn't work. Granted, Mattie wasn't really playing Trevor. Maybe Agent Shezza was actually too smart, not too stupid.

"You're the one who—" *SLAP*.

Nah. She was definitely stupid. This wasn't going to work.

Then Tillie had a new idea. A new plan. She tried to switch into seer mode, but apparently, her magical abilities were frozen along with her body. She wouldn't have time to check things through once she was no longer frozen - she'd have to act fast.

Suddenly, Tillie found herself unfrozen and falling off-balance. She stumbled forward and crashed into Trevor who had leaped forward to catch her.

"Thank you," said Mattie.

"I didn't—" Agent Shezza sounded completely bewildered.

The glow of Mattie's hands pulsed and the Auditor's lips froze back up mid-word.

Tillie spared a moment of sympathy as she rolled her shoulders and stretched her aching limbs. Being frozen was a lot worse than it looked.

Then she launched herself at Mattie, tackling her to the ground.

4.

Mattie crashed to the ground, her head narrowly missing the corner of the coffee table and thankfully hitting a cushion that had somehow tumbled to the ground beside it, her limbs tangled up in her sister's.

"What the fuck?" she yelped.

"This plan isn't working," hissed Tillie. "I'm moving on to something else."

"What are you talking about?" Mattie gasped.

"Keep your voice down," Tillie whispered. "This won't work if she hears us. Pretend we're fighting."

Mattie rolled herself and Tillie toward the kitchen, away from the prisoner, doing her best to keep them in the frozen woman's field of vision while moving farther out of earshot.

"Perfect," said Tillie. "Now I'm going to get the upper hand and then pretend to knock you out. Play along and then once you're 'out,' release the Auditor from your spell."

"What? Why?"

"Just do it!"

"Okay, fine." Mattie rolled again, putting her sister on top of the fake scuffle.

Tillie jumped to her feet and aimed a kick at Mattie's head.

It just brushed her ear, and she breathed a sigh of relief that her sister's control was on point. If she had been just a little bit to the right, she might have actually knocked her out.

Mattie closed her eyes and went limp, releasing the spell holding the Auditor frozen as she did so.

She heard a scuffle and her sister yelled, "Let me go! What are you—"

And then Trevor. "Oh, shit! Wait!"

Mattie's eyes snapped open. Tillie and the Auditor were nowhere to be seen.

Sitting up, she rubbed her arm where Tillie had squeezed a little hard when she'd tackled her. "What's going on? What did she do?"

Trevor turned and locked eyes with Mattie. "She got herself kidnapped."

"What?" Mattie jumped to her feet. "Again?"

"Well, no," said Trevor. "Technically, this is the first time she's actually been kidnapped. We thought she had been before, but she had just run away, remember?"

Mattie stared at him. "So what?"

"I don't know," he admitted. "I just like to keep the facts straight."

The door opened and Giovani and Ida ambled in. "Whoa, what happened here?" said Giovani, looking around.

Mattie looked around too and realized that the usually-pristine room was in a bit of a shambles, the coffee table askew and an armchair knocked over sideways onto the floor.

"My fucking sister just up and got herself disappeared again!" Mattie said.

Ida tsked. "That one is a trouble-maker. Nice girl, but once you get that taste of adventure, you just can't sit still, I suppose. Well, you go looking for trouble, you're sure to find it, I always say."

"Why did she run off this time?" asked Giovani.

"She's been kidnapped," Trevor corrected.

"Sort of," said Mattie.

"How can someone be sort of kidnapped?" Ida raised one of her thick eyebrows. "And is there any tea to be had before we get into this story?"

"I made a pot this morning. Earl Grey." Mattie nodded toward the kitchen and Ida headed in that direction.

Mattie picked up the green armchair and set it back upright. She turned to fix the rakish angle of the coffee table, but Trevor was already on it. "Thanks," she said. She sat down on the chair with a sigh. Then she stood up again, remembering that a man had died on it just yesterday.

She moved to the couch.

"Is there a problem with the chair?" said Giovani.

"It's creepy," Mattie muttered. "Anyway, I think we'd better wait for Ida."

The three of them sat for a moment, awkwardly looking at each other.

Ida bustled back into the living room, setting a tea tray on the coffee table with mugs for everyone. Mattie hoped there was enough tea left – she had already had one cup this morning and couldn't remember if Tillie had drunk any of it too.

She grabbed a mug and poured herself a cup of the earl grey tea, adding half-and-half and then settling back down on the couch, sipping it contentedly as Ida and Trevor served themselves as well.

"All right," said Giovani. "You've all got your precious tea. Now, what happened?"

"We were on our way down to Tillie's storage unit," Mattie began. "And this Auditor attacked us. Agent Shezza."

Giovani groaned.

Mattie's eyebrows shot up. "You know her?"

"Yeah, I know her," he admitted. "She's an idiot. And incredibly brainwashed."

"Yes," Mattie agreed. "She seemed very intent on making sure we both knew that we were abominations, even though, technically, I'm not one."

"She called me one too," Trevor said. "I wouldn't take it personally."

"Like I said, she's an idiot," said Giovani. "Please go on."

"Right. So I did a spell and made her freeze, so she couldn't move or talk or anything and we brought her up here and Tillie had this idea to do a good-cop/bad-cop situation so we could convince her that I was on her side and maybe she'd tell us where to find the whatchamacallit – the court."

"I doubt she'd even know," said Giovani. "That's not really commonly shared with field agents unless they're being disciplined or commended."

"Okay, well that would have been good to know," said Mattie, shooting a glare in his direction.

He threw up his hands. "Look, there's a lot of information that would be good for you to know, but I am only one man, and you guys interrupt a lot!"

"Well, you're the one interrupting this time," said Ida. "Go on, dear."

"Thank you." Mattie shook her head, trying to collect her thoughts. "Where was I?"

"Good-cop/bad-cop," said Trevor.

"Right. So, it's not working, because she's totally convinced that we're both abominations, even though, again, I'm definitely not one —"

"You don't need to convince us, dear," said Ida. "We don't think you're an abomination."

"We don't even think Tillie is an abomination," said Trevor.

"Nor Giovani," added Ida with a smile to her nephew. "An idiot maybe. But not an abomination."

"Does anyone else think that 'abomination' doesn't even sound like a real word anymore?" said Mattie.

"Oh, for fuck's sake, you guys have got to focus!" said Giovani, squeezing his eyes shut. He looked stressed out, and Mattie remembered what he had said the day before about his anxiety issues.

"Right. Yes." Mattie took a deep breath and tried to focus on where she'd been in her story again. Oh, yeah. Good-cop/bad-cop. "So she's not getting my whole I'm-on-your-side schtick, even when Trevor comes in and demands that she release Tillie and I'm pretending that she's the one with the spell and trying to give her hints that she should play along so that I can be a 'double agent.' It's just completely over her head. So I release Tillie anyway and that's when Tillie goes off on her own plan that she apparently —"

"I'm sorry, dear, I'm a little bit lost," interrupted Ida. "Release Tillie from what?"

"Oh, yeah, part of my good-cop thing was to put Tillie in a freeze-spell too."

Ida nodded. "Thank you. That was good thinking. Too bad it didn't work, but you can't rely on the reactions of everyone around you, I always say."

"Especially morons," muttered Giovani.

Mattie suppressed a smile. Good to know that she wasn't the only one annoyed by Agent Shezza's lack of intelligence. "So, Tillie straight-up tackles me and tells me to play along and that she's going to pretend to knock me out and when she does to release Agent Shezza from the spell, and so I do all that, but of course my eyes are closed, so I really have no idea what happened next, except that they both disappeared."

"Well, my eyes were open," said Trevor.

"Oh, yeah, you were here at that point," said Mattie.

"Thanks for noticing," said Trevor, wryly. "So, about an hour ago, Tillie texted me and asked me to come over early. She told me that they had another Auditor in custody and asked me to come barging in and demand that Mattie release her. Then she said that they had a big plan they were working through and that it was too much to really explain via text, so if I could just do my thing and then step aside and let it all play out, that'd be great.

"So I did that, but as Mattie said, it didn't work out, but I didn't actually know it wasn't working, because I didn't know what was supposed to happen. After she tackled Mattie, Tillie rushed straight at the Auditor and her lips were moving and her hands were glowing. I honestly have no idea what kind of spell she was doing – nothing around her was moving or changing, but she was clearly spelling. And then Agent Shezza grabbed her arm and stitched them both out of there."

Ida cackled. "Smart girl! I bet it was just a nonsense spell with no real effects – maybe moving a cushion around or something."

"You mean she was just trying to bait her?" said Mattie. "She got herself kidnapped on purpose. Now we have a woman on the inside! She's brilliant!"

"She is not brilliant!" Giovani leaped to his feet, raking his hands through his sandy hair. "What the hell was she thinking? We all spent the last two weeks desperately trying to keep her from being taken by the Auditors and what does she do as soon as the going gets tough? She gets herself taken by the Auditors!"

"Well, this is different," said Mattie. Wasn't it?

Giovani pivoted toward her and she involuntarily pressed herself against the back of the couch. Damn, that guy was scary when he was mad.

"How?" he demanded. "How is this different? Please, enlighten me!"

Mattie narrowed her eyes and deliberately leaned forward, refusing to be intimidated for more than a moment. "It's different because she's in control of the situation."

"Is she?" Giovani shook his head. "Does she have any idea what she's in for right now?"

"She's a seer," Trevor pointed out. "She must have looked forward and found it worth the risk."

Ida cleared her throat.

Mattie turned to face her.

"Dear, did your spell leave her eyes moveable?" Ida asked Mattie, gently.

"I don't know." Mattie frowned. "I'm still new at this. I guess my intent was that they'd still be alive, so presumably, their lungs and hearts still worked, but I didn't build anything into it about eyes, no."

"So her seer ability was not available," concluded Giovani. He sank back onto the couch and rubbed his hands over his face. "She just jumped right in, like a speller would. Which is another thing I should probably mention. A side effect of all this morphing."

"Morphing?" said Trevor. "What is that?"

"That's what I've started calling this learning-other-disciplines thing, ever since —" Giovani cut himself off, his lips pursing. His nostrils flared as he inhaled sharply.

Mattie's eyes narrowed. What wasn't Giovani telling them?

"Ever since....?" she prompted.

"It's what I was going to tell you yesterday. What my son said that made me begin to question the integrity and, you know, the rightness of the organization." He paused. "Maybe I should back up."

"Oh, hurry up and get on with it," said Mattie. "Just spit it out! What did your son say and what do we really need to know before we can get on with the rescue mission?"

He grimaced. "I'll sum it up. Basically, Marco told me that the higher-ups in the Pontiff's court, including the Pontiff himself, practiced something called 'morphing.' He was excited because he was going to be allowed to start morphing lessons soon. When pressed, he explained that morphing was 'stretching out your mage senses into new areas of expertise.' Which sounds a lot like what they like to call 'abomination.' And what you need to know before you try to rescue Tillie is that there's no fucking way you're going to be able to do so."

5.

Tillie sat up groggily and tried to remember the events that had led her to this padded cell. It wasn't white, so she was pretty sure that meant she wasn't in a mental institute. Or at least not the kind she'd seen on TV.

So, where the hell was she? She closed her eyes and breathed in deeply, deliberately calming herself with her steady breathing. Opening her eyes again, she moved them into seer mode.

Nothing happened.

She moved her eyes back to normal sight mode and then back to seer mode again.

The world remained as it had been – a small grey room with no furniture, just a cushiony material covering the walls, floor, and low ceiling.

No comforting overlay of future possibilities. The walls didn't take on that slight translucency that would show her what was outside of them and who might be coming toward her.

Maybe if she tried further forward.

Nothing.

Tillie's breathing began to hitch as she started to panic. What the hell had she been thinking, jumping into this?

Maybe if she tried a spell instead.

Shrieking a Latin word, Tillie flung her hands toward the door, trying to open it. Her hands refused to glow and the door remained resolutely shut.

"No," she whimpered. She had discovered magic at a low point in her life, and it had saved her. It had been a constant for her ever since, bolstering her confidence and helping her feel powerful enough to navigate whatever came her way.

Without magic, who was she? Just an ordinary woman? The world was not kind to ordinary women. She couldn't go back to that.

Her legs kicked compulsively, and she scooted backward until she was pressed into a corner of the room.

Going nowhere.

Tillie began to sob quietly.

6.

Mattie leaped to her feet. "Those fucking hypocrites!"

"Exactly," said Giovani.

"I'm sorry, could you back the fuck up a little?" said Trevor. "When you say 'there's no fucking way,' you mean…?"

"I mean it's impossible," said Giovani. "One hundred percent, absolutely not going to happen."

"That seems a little bit—" Ida began.

"No!" Giovani turned toward his aunt, breathing heavily, his face twisted in despair. "I know you have some positive adage, some catchy thing that you 'always say,' some encouraging bit of meaningless drivel, but the fact is that Tillie is now in the hands of an ancient, evil organization that will stop at nothing to maintain its own power, and she is about to become part of it and she's never coming out."

He gasped for air and wrapped his arms around himself tightly, his panic visibly growing by the moment.

Mattie sat down abruptly, staring at Giovani, unsure how to handle his anxiety attack.

"You came out," said Trevor, quietly.

"That's—"

"Different?" said Trevor. "You're right. It is different. You had no help."

"Yes, but—"

"Everyone had already given up on you," added Ida. "When I was looking for you, I didn't know anything about who had taken you."

"And you didn't know anything either," pointed out Mattie.

"Neither does Tillie!" Giovani slammed his fist into the coffee table. His anxiety seemed to have channeled itself into anger, which seemed to Mattie to be a vast improvement. "That's what I've been trying to explain! Does Tillie know who the Auditors are? Yes. Does she know what their mission is? Sure. Does she know anything about what they're about to do to her? Absolutely not! These people are good at what they do because they've been doing it for over a thousand years."

He slumped in his chair. "Do you understand the vastness of that number? This organization is old."

"And it's rotting from the inside out," said Trevor. "We're looking at this the wrong way. This organization is old."

"I just said that," said Giovani. He sounded worn out.

"Yes, but look at what we've learned from these two agents who've attacked us over the past couple of days. They're rebelling against the court. And they're not the only ones. It sounds like Agent Miller was leading a coup. Can we use that to our advantage?" Trevor paused. "How did your son know about the court morphing?"

"His court mentor told him," said Giovani. "He's being taught the basics of it."

"Your son has a court mentor?" said Mattie.

"That's what the court is," explained Giovani. "Anytime agents have children, they're automatically inducted into the court. And, of course, children of court-members as well."

"So, how many people are there in this court?" Trevor frowned.

"Not as many as you'd think," Giovani said. "Maybe a few hundred. There's just as much backstabbing and assassination as they jockey for power as there is producing new ones. It kind of evens out."

"And this is where my great-nephew is growing up?" Ida scowled.

"He's only eight," said Giovani. "He won't be assassinated yet."

"Yet?" she yelled, lunging for his throat.

Mattie hastily flung up a shield, wishing Scott had agreed to come back today. If this was going to keep happening, she really didn't want to be the only speller between Ida and Giovani.

But Scott had decided that he wouldn't have anything to do with a coup. Pacifism again.

"Ida!" said Trevor, grabbing her arm and holding her back. "You have to stop attacking Giovani or we're never going to get anything done!"

She subsided reluctantly. "You're right, I suppose."

"We'll rescue him and the other kids," promised Giovani.

"How many kids are there?" asked Mattie.

"Honestly? I don't know. Probably a couple hundred," said Giovani.

"And what are we going to do with a couple hundred kids?" asked Mattie. "I can tell you right now, I'm not taking care of them."

"One thing at a time, please," said Trevor. "We need a plan. Giovani. How did you find Tillie before? How did you know to show up in Seattle?"

"I called her. But I see where you're going with that. I, ah, borrowed Mattie's phone, you'll recall."

"Stole," corrected Mattie.

"Well, I gave it back," he pointed out. "Anyway, I used a combination of spelling, stitching, and a scrying bowl to get Tillie's current phone number from her old one." Giovani sighed and ran a hand over his already-rumpled hair. "It was not easy. That was one of the first times I ever used all three disciplines in tandem."

"She doesn't have a phone with her, I suppose," said Ida.

"What was she wearing?" said Trevor. "If she had a pocket, I guarantee she had her phone with her."

"And if she did, I guarantee it's been taken away," countered Giovani.

"She was in work-out gear anyway," said Mattie. "No pockets."

"How did the Auditors track her?" said Trevor. "She told me that they always seemed to manage to find her, even though she was hitching rides and staying in roadside motels that never even asked her for ID. She was using fake names and switching them up every time. They had to have used magic to track her, right?"

"Sure," said Giovani. "That was part of why we always worked in pairs. You'd have a speller and a stitcher or a stitcher and a seer, and then we'd work together to use the combination to track the target's magical signature."

"So, why can't we do that?" said Mattie. "We have all of those right here."

"Because the organization will have her behind shields that dampen her magic," he said. "No magic, no signature."

Of course. "Wait, so she can't use her magic at all? Not even her seer abilities?" Mattie's eyes widened. "She's going to be completely lost."

"That's what I've been trying to tell you," said Giovani. "She's totally screwed. There's no way we can help her. There's no way she can help herself. At best, we'll have to wait until she's finished with her conditioning. At that point, they'll start training her to be an agent. She'll have full use of her magic – only the seeing, of course, but that's all she'll want to use anyway. And they'll let her move freely around whatever city she's in, outside of their shielded buildings. At that point, we may be able to grab her, but by then she'll have to be unbrainwashed."

"Okay, so how long do we have to wait?" said Mattie.

"One year."

7.

Tillie's sobs quieted and her mind slowly began to calm itself. She forced herself to breathe evenly again and wiped the tears from her face. Eyes closed, she moved her limbs into a lotus and focused on her breathing, working her way through familiar breathwork exercises.

Magic or no magic, she was no ordinary woman, after all. She had evaded the Auditors before.

Barely, whispered a little voice inside. *And only because Giovani helped and Mattie and Trevor swooped in at the last minute.*

Tillie pushed the thought aside and cleared her mind once more. She inhaled positivity and exhaled doubts. She was Tillie Holiday. A strong woman with other skills besides magic. Krav maga. Fabulous taste. Incredibly organized. Always prepared for every eventuality.

And she had planned this! She hadn't really been kidnapped. She had gone willingly, deliberately. She had tricked that idiot Agent Shezza. Maybe it hadn't been the most well-thought-through plan she'd ever had, but it was about time she started acting like the woman behind the whole scheme and not the victim of it.

She had promised herself years ago that she would never be a victim again. And Tillie Holiday didn't make promises she couldn't keep.

Tillie opened her eyes and smiled. After all, even without magical sight, she still had the planning ability of a natural seer. She unbuttoned the pocket of her deep blue cardigan and pulled out her cell phone.

8.

The living room of Tillie's condo erupted into chaos as everyone jumped to their feet and began shouting at once. As soon as Mattie realized she wasn't going to be heard, she stopped yelling and began to try to listen to what everyone else was saying instead.

Ida was yelling about Giovani's kid again and how she wasn't leaving him in the clutches of those evil motherfuckers for another day, much less a year.

Trevor was shouting similar things about Tillie.

Giovani was shouting that if Tillie had just waited for him to arrive, they wouldn't be in this mess to begin with.

And underneath all of it, Mattie could hear a phone ringing. It sounded like hers. Was it hers? She couldn't quite hear it.

Where was her phone anyway?

She patted her pockets. Not there. She had it in the kitchen this morning. It must be in there.

Mattie gently pushed Trevor aside and dodged Ida's wagging finger as she passed between the old woman and her nephew. As she neared the kitchen, the phone got louder.

Excellent – it *was* in there.

She picked it up off the counter and stared at it in shock. Then she shook herself and hit the answer button. "Tillie? Tillie, is that really you?"

"Mattie!" Her sister's voice filled with relief. "Oh, my god! I'm so happy to hear your voice! I can't use my magic! I may have bitten off more than I can chew. I'm sorry."

"That's okay! Hold on a sec!" Mattie ran back into the living room and began shoving her compatriots back into their respective seats. They quieted down as she did so, glaring at her.

"What?" said Giovani.

"It's Tillie!" hissed Mattie. "She has her phone after all!"

"I told you so!" said Trevor.

"Go ahead, Tillie." Mattie hit the speaker button and turned the phone to face the room.

" —have me in this weird little padded room with nothing in it."

"Wait, what?" Giovani frowned. "You're sure? You're in a cell?"

"Well, yeah, I'm sure. I'm here."

"Is that not standard?" asked Mattie.

He ignored her. "Is the cell grey?"

"Yes. And padded all over, even the floor."

"Alone?" he persisted.

"Yes, completely."

"And you weren't searched?"

"I guess not. I must have blanked out. Maybe I was drugged. I don't remember. How long have I been gone?"

"Not long enough," said Giovani. "I mean, you should be on a train right now with a guard. Not in a cell. And if you're in a cell already, that means they're keeping you in St. Louis. We may have a chance to get you out before they start conditioning."

"I have to go." Tillie's voice was suddenly tense.

"What? Why?" Mattie turned the phone toward her just in time to see those fateful words, *Call Ended.* "She hung up."

"That's okay," said Giovani, standing. "Let's go. We need to act fast."

Mattie grabbed her bag off the coat tree near the door. "Where are we going?"

"Every major city in America has an Auditor HQ," said Giovani. He strode to the door and held it open for everyone to file out.

Mattie paused to lock the condo door and then followed down the stairs.

"That must be where they have her. It's highly irregular that she's being held in the same city in which she was captured. I don't know why they would do that. Why did they decide to keep her in St. Louis?"

"Maybe they didn't," said Trevor.

"There hasn't been time—" said Giovani.

"No, I'm saying maybe it's not 'them,'" suggested Trevor. "Maybe the Auditors don't have her. Maybe Agent Miller's splinter group does. Maybe Agent Shezza isn't following protocol anymore."

Giovani stopped walking and Mattie smacked right into his back.

"Sorry," she muttered.

"But then I don't know where she is," he said.

"You said it sounded like an Auditor cell, right?" said Trevor. "Grey, padded, empty?"

"Sure."

"Then she probably did take her to Auditor HQ. But maybe the rest of the Auditors don't know about her yet."

"So let's go!" said Mattie, stamping her foot for emphasis. "Before they find out!"

9.

Tillie hastily returned her phone to her pocket, buttoning it up and then pulling herself to her feet as the key scraped in the lock. She stared defiantly at the woman who slipped into the room. It wasn't Agent Shezza, but another agent, tall and slender with a sureness about her movements that told Tillie that she would be a formidable physical opponent.

The other woman squatted briefly to set a tray of food down on the floor and then straightened, leaning back against the door, arms crossed, and studied Tillie in kind.

"Well," she said, finally. "I suppose you think you're very clever."

Tillie frowned. "Do I?"

"You do not have my permission to speak."

"I don't need it," Tillie retorted.

"Fair enough." A slight smile flitted across the Auditor's lips. "You've got grit. I like it. My name is Agent Poe, and you and I will be getting to know each other quite well."

The woman picked up the tray of food again and left the room with it, locking the door behind her.

"Well, that was rude," Tillie muttered. She was hungry. It had already been a long day, and it was still pretty early. That smoothie had only been about an hour and a half ago, but it felt a lot longer. "Guess I'll just have to go and find something to eat."

Tillie examined the door. She tried the knob. She'd heard the woman lock it, but you never knew. Sometimes people turned the key the wrong way or turned it back again. Never rule out basic human incompetence.

In this case, however, the door was locked. Twice. She noted there was a basic lock on the knob and a sturdier deadbolt above it.

She automatically muttered the phrase for an unlocking spell. It didn't work. Right. No magic. No worries. She was a sex worker, after all – she always had plenty of resources for when a situation went very wrong.

Unbuttoning her cardigan pocket again, Tillie pulled out her phone and pried up the corner of its bulky case, revealing a variety of useful items sandwiched between the case and the phone. She selected a flat tool that unfolded into various sized lockpicks.

A small smile tugging at her lips, she got to work on the deadbolt. It was always best to start with the tougher task. Get it out of the way and the simpler one would feel that much easier.

10.

Mattie held her breath as Giovani entered a code on the keypad beside the door of a nondescript stone building in Midtown. She released it in a whoosh as the door slid open silently. Giovani stepped inside, followed by Trevor and Ida.

Mattie glanced around the alley once more and then followed. She jumped as the door slid closed behind her. "I feel like I'm in a fucking spaceship," she muttered.

"The organization has resources," Giovani murmured. "Never underestimate them."

"Well, then they'll be that much more filled with hubris and overconfidence," said Ida, cheerfully. "I'm not used to being an underdog, but I can get the hang of it, I suppose. The key should be to use their size against them, right? Metaphorically speaking, I mean. The actual people will be normal-sized, I suppose."

"Normal size, yes, but very physically fit for the most part, well-trained in the martial art of their preference, and very devoted to their cause," Giovani cautioned. "Well, the agents anyway. The court will be guarded by agents. And there are some court-members trained as guards, and some who practice combat magic for competitions."

"I don't care about the court right now," said Trevor. "We need to rescue Tillie before she gets brainwashed or taken elsewhere."

"I'm gonna call her," said Mattie, pulling out her phone. "Maybe she can tell us where she is."

"No!" Giovani and Trevor spun around together, arms outstretched to stop her.

"Whoa! Hey!" Mattie lifted her hands in surrender. "Why not?"

"She hung up on you for a reason," said Trevor. "Do you want her captors to find out she has her phone? Let her call us when she's ready."

"And put your phone on vibrate," said Giovani. "We also don't want to alert anyone else that we're here."

"Fair enough." Mattie changed her settings. "Now what? Where would she be held?"

"I mean, I know where —" Giovani broke off. "Shhhh." He flattened himself against the wall. "Someone's coming."

"And your solution is to look like you're up to no good?" Mattie rolled her eyes. She jerked her head toward an open door to their left. "Come on. In here."

Mattie poked her head into the room and found it empty of people, so she walked in and looked around.

"Nice! A library!" said Trevor. He walked to the closest bookcase and pulled down a thick volume. "*On the Psychology of the Abomination: Why They Begin the Path of Destruction*. Heavy reading."

Mattie giggled. "The Auditors have their own publishing companies?"

"Of course they do," said Giovani. "The organization is a fully off-grid, fully formed society that functions completely separately from the outside world."

"Quiet! Here they come!" Ida, standing by the door, turned and shushed them. "Everyone act natural!"

Mattie grabbed another book at random and sat down at one of the long tables arranged in the middle of the room. The others joined her.

She opened the book in front of her and stared at the page.

The abomination will be defiant, but disoriented. In almost every case, the abomination has no idea they have done wrong. Remember your own experience and draw upon that. Remember the tough love shown to you by your recruitment agents and bestow the same upon your new recruit. We must show them the error of their ways and guide them to better ways.

Mattie wrinkled her nose. What kind of cultish bullshit was this?

She was saved from more reading as a man entered the room.

"Garaveldi!" The newcomer hailed Giovani and Mattie tensed. Just their luck – the very first Auditor they encounter recognized him.

She forced herself to relax. The man seemed jovial enough. Maybe he didn't know that Giovani had switched sides.

"Bachman!" Giovani stood and greeted the man, clapping him on the back convivially. "It's been a while!"

Thank goodness for that. Mattie smiled in relief.

The Auditor looked around at the rest of them. "And some newbies, I see?" His gaze lingered on Ida, a puzzled frown forming.

Uh oh. Maybe it had been a mistake to bring her along. There probably weren't a lot of agents in their eighties. It was a high-risk career.

Giovani cleared his throat and swept an arm toward his aunt. "Actually, may I present Her Grace, the Duchess of Shielding?"

"Oh!" The man's eyes widened. "My apologies – I forgot about the pending occupation. Here to check out the fortifications, I guess? I can assure you, this HQ is in top shape."

"I'll be the judge of that, young man," Ida said, sharply. She lifted an imperious arm, gesturing toward the door. "Agent Bachman, was it? Do you have duties to attend to?"

He jumped, guiltily. "Yeah, yes, of course! I'll just go and finish my perimeter check. Thank you, Your Grace." He backed out of the room.

Mattie giggled, meeting Trevor's dancing eyes.

"Your Grace!" laughed Ida. "Oh, I like that."

"Is 'Duchess of Shielding' a real thing?" asked Mattie. "What a ridiculous title!"

"It might be," Giovani shrugged. "I know that the court bestows titles based on areas of expertise rather than geography. I'm more interested in that comment he made about the 'pending occupation.'"

"What does that mean?" Trevor asked.

"It means the court is coming here," said Giovani. "We might have just stumbled upon the lucky break of the century. The viper's head on a silver platter."

11.

There! Tillie felt the second lock's tumblers release at last. It had been a while since she'd had to pick a lock, but the skills had come rushing back after a minute or two.

She turned the knob and cautiously opened the door a crack. It jerked to a halt and she realized that there was also a chain lock. Dammit! Her picks weren't going to do any good against that.... Did she have a rubber band on her? Any escort worth her salt knew how to break out of or into a hotel room, and the best way to disarm a chain lock was with a rubber band.

Tillie quickly sorted through her pockets. No rubber band in her cell phone case, nor loose in her pockets. She pulled off her sneakers and removed their insoles, finding two prepaid credit cards, a spare key to her condo, and a couple more odds and ends.

No rubber bands. As she started to put her shoes back on, she paused. Could a shoelace work?

Tillie quickly unlaced her shoe and slid the string through the cracked door, carefully weaving it into the chain. She saw the problem immediately – a rubber band would stretch to reach the door handle. The shoelace wasn't long enough.

No problem. Tillie unlaced the other shoe and tied the laces together. She held her breath as she pulled the end toward the knob. It reached, but barely. Good – it would be plenty taut to tug at the chain.

Slowly, careful not to tug too hard and unravel it, she wrapped the end around the knob.

Slowly, she closed the door, listening for the sound of the chain pulling across its track. It sounded good....

She closed her eyes and took a deep breath. Then she opened the door. All the way. The chain was gone! Yes!

Tillie grinned and unwound her shoelaces from the chain. She turned and grabbed her shoes, surveying the cell to make sure she wasn't leaving anything behind. She stepped out into the hallway and closed the door behind her.

Glancing up and down the corridor, she saw that it was lined with doors on one side – presumably cells just like the one she'd just left – and benches on the other. Tillie sat down on a bench and relaced her shoes, considering her next move. Experimentally, she tried switching into seer mode once again. No luck. So the anti-magic shields extended past the individual cells.

Well, she'd gotten this far without it; she could manage a little longer. She considered her options.

She could explore this part of the building further. Maybe there were other prisoners in the cells who could be allies. Then again, if the others in the cells had been there longer, they might be already brainwashed into calling in the Auditors. High risk, high reward? Maybe.

Tillie wished she knew more about who would be kept in a cell. Surely the more advanced recruits would be in a dormitory or something, right? These would be the raw abominations like her.

What were the alternatives? She could explore the rest of the building, pretend to be a fully-fledged agent, infiltrate the ranks. Wasn't that what she'd wanted to do in the first place? That's why she'd gotten herself kidnapped – to be the inside woman.

She finished relacing her shoes and tied them up neatly. Then she pulled out her phone again. A good spy should be in touch with the rest of her crew, after all.

She called Mattie. It rang and rang and then went to voicemail.

Hanging up, she tried Trevor. Same deal.

Giovani's went straight to voicemail.

Did Ida have a cell? Probably not. She was eighty-two. Tillie shrugged. Didn't matter if she had one or not – she didn't have the number.

She typed in a quick text to Mattie and Trevor and sent it. *Escaped my cell. Planning to infiltrate Auditor ranks. Catch you later.*

Slipping her phone back into her pocket, Tillie set off down the hallway toward a promising-looking set of heavy double-doors.

12.

The group split up at Giovani's suggestion. He'd said smaller groups would be less conspicuous. Mattie and Trevor strode down the hall, confidence in every line of their bodies, exuding the sense that they belonged. Mattie hoped it was working.

It seemed like it was. No one had stopped them anyway. Actually, everyone seemed to be in a big hurry, scurrying around the building on important missions of their own, barely glancing at her. She wondered if that's how it always was or if it was because they were getting ready for the Pontiff and his court.

Their mission was to find and free Tillie. Hopefully, before she got all brainwashed or whatever. She'd only been there for an hour or so. How much brainwashing could happen in that time?

"Here," said Trevor. He pointed to a door with a picture of a staircase on it. "Giovani said the cells would be in the basement."

"Perfect." Mattie shoved her way into the stairwell. "Or not."

The stairs only went up.

"Maybe there's an elevator," suggested Trevor.

"Pretty sure they have to have stairs," Mattie objected. "For fire codes and stuff, right?"

"I don't think a secret society is all that concerned about fire codes."

"Yeah, but the building exists in this city. Don't they have to at least pretend it's a business or something?" Mattie frowned. "How the hell does a secret society actually run under the radar in this day and age when there are records for everything?"

"I'm guessing the government has other things to worry about," said Trevor. "Either way, this is a dead end."

Mattie pushed the door open again and wandered back out into the hallway. "I guess we keep looking, then."

A passing woman paused. "What are you looking for?"

"The basement," said Mattie. "The prison cells."

The woman cocked her head. "Certainly. For what purpose, Agent...?"

"Holiday," Mattie supplied. "We're checking out the security. Making sure none of the abominations can get out." She gestured toward Trevor. "This is the, uh, Count of Prison Guards."

"Oh!" The woman straightened her spine and saluted. "It's an honor, my lord. Right this way!"

"Great," said Mattie. "Thank you."

She and Trevor exchanged grins as the Auditor turned on her heel and began to lead them down the corridor.

Trevor nudged her and whispered. "I think 'The Count of Prison Guards' is going to be my new username on all online accounts from here on out."

"Don't let it go to your head," Mattie whispered back.

"My lord?" Their guide had stopped in front of a new door, and Mattie and Trevor hastened to catch up with her. "Through this door, you'll find the way down. I hope you'll forgive me if I don't accompany you – I have a lot to do to prepare for the rest of the court."

"Of course," said Trevor. "No problem. Thank you for your assistance."

"I am Agent Poe. I hope you'll remember me well." Agent Poe's face had on an odd expression, almost as though she were trying to hold back some emotion.

Mattie wondered what it was.

"Of course," said Trevor again.

Mattie followed him through the door and it slammed behind them. She felt a sudden pang of unease, but couldn't quite put her finger on why. She shrugged it off.

They descended a short flight of stairs with a set of heavy double doors at the bottom.

Trevor pushed against the right-hand side, depressing the silver bar handle, but the door didn't open.

"Try the other side," Mattie suggested.

"Thanks, I know how doors work," he said, dryly.

"Oh, good."

He smirked at her as he turned and pushed against the other side with his back.

It didn't open either.

"Is there a keypad?" Mattie frowned and looked around. "Or maybe there's a key. I bet the real Count of Prison Guards has a key."

"Agent Poe didn't say anything about a key," Trevor pointed out.

"That's because she thought you were a real count. And would therefore have the key." Mattie rolled her eyes. "Come on, let's go see if she's still around. We can tell her you left it in your countal robes or something."

"Countal?"

"I don't know! This is America! I don't know anything about actual counts!" Mattie jogged back up the steps and pressed the bar on the door at the top. "Uh oh. That shitsucker!"

"What?" Trevor stepped up beside her.

"It's not opening either. She locked us in!"

"Let me try." He nudged her aside.

"Look, I know how doors work too!" Nevertheless, she stepped back. She raised her eyebrows as he tried the door. "See? It's locked. The question is whether Poe knew this would happen."

"Why would she lock a count in a stairwell?" Trevor protested.

"Because I told her you were the Count of Prison Guards!" Mattie deflated. "What a ridiculous title!"

Trevor shrugged. "Don't beat yourself up, Matts. It's no weirder than the Duchess of Shields and that other dude bought that."

"I feel like it's a little weirder," Mattie muttered. She did feel somewhat better, though. "Okay, how do we get out of here? Do you think banging on the door is a good idea?"

"Hmm." Trevor frowned and lifted his hands, palms up like a scale. "On the one hand, if we are believable as the Count of Prison Guards and his bodyguard, it would be effective. On the other, if we're not, then we're drawing more attention to ourselves."

"What if Agent Poe is bringing reinforcements?" said Mattie.

"And this is our holding cell," Trevor finished. "Very possible."

"Okay, but which is most likely?" Mattie huffed in frustration. "Why the hell did we split off from Giovani? He's the only one of us who knows how to navigate this fucking place!"

Trevor lifted a finger to his lips and Mattie froze.

A creak came from below. The door was opening.

13.

Tillie pushed open the door at the end of the hallway and peeked out. It looked like a stairwell. She glanced up the stairs and froze as she saw two shadowy figures pressed against the wall at the top.

Then she squinted and breathed a sigh of relief. "Trevor! Mattie!" she called up. "Am I glad to see you!"

Mattie leaned forward and stared at her. "Tillie?"

"How'd you find me?"

"We didn't so much find you as stumble upon you," said Trevor. He skipped down the steps and flung an arm around her shoulders, squeezing her warmly.

Tillie turned to Mattie, who had followed Trevor down and was now peering out the door into the hall Tillie had just left. "What's the plan?"

"Find you," said Mattie.

Tillie raised an eyebrow. "And then?"

"Rescue you," said Mattie.

Tillie rolled her eyes. "Okay, well, I've already rescued myself. So, what now?"

Trevor grinned sheepishly. "You could maybe rescue us? We got ourselves locked in a stairwell."

She sighed. "Okay, so, what's the end game?"

"Take down the Auditors," said Mattie.

Tillie looked at her sister with exasperation.

Mattie grinned back.

"Any thoughts for what might happen in between rescuing me and taking down the organization?"

"So far, it's just getting locked in a stairwell," said Trevor. "Giovani and Ida are running some reconnaissance too."

"Ah, well, that's good news," said Tillie, sarcastically. Why was she running around with these people who couldn't plan anything if their lives depended on it? Actually, come to think of it, their lives *did* depend on it. And yet, here they were. "Do you have a way to get ahold of them?"

"Well, yeah," said Mattie. "This is the twenty-first century. We have cell phones."

"Do you plan on answering them ever?" said Tillie, sweetly. "Because I called all three of you about ten minutes ago and no one picked up."

"Dammit! We put them on silent!" Mattie dug in her pocket and pulled out her phone. "Yep, there it is. Missed call and a text from you. And a missed call from Giovani. Oh, you're free. Good."

Tillie waited. She raised an eyebrow. "Did Giovani leave a message?"

"No. I'll just call him back."

Tillie sighed again, watching with steadily eroding patience as Mattie held her phone up to her ear.

She glanced at Trevor. "I expect better from you, love," she said quietly. But she smiled to show she didn't mean it. Well, that she only sort of meant it anyway.

He smiled back, wryly. "It's all been moving so fast, Tills. I don't operate that way. I need you to plan for me."

"I'm here now." She grabbed his hand and squeezed it. He squeezed it back, and all was right with the world.

"Well, he didn't answer," said Mattie. "I texted him that we'd found you. Hopefully, he'll get back to me with a rendezvous point."

"A rendezvous point? So you have a map of the building or some kind of idea of how to get around?" said Tillie.

"Well, no."

"Seriously, Tills," said Trevor. "We really need you!"

"Okay, okay." She beckoned with both hands. "Lay it on me. Everything that's happened since I left."

Tillie listened intently as Trevor ran through their past couple of hours.

"And then we were in the stairwell for just a minute or so before you popped in and now we're all in here," he finished.

Tillie pursed her lips. "It would have been nice to know that this door locked from the inside from the start."

"I've been holding it open," protested Mattie. Sure enough, her foot was stuck in the door, keeping it ajar.

"And your magic isn't working either, I assume?" said Tillie.

"Your magic isn't working?" said Mattie.

Tillie closed her eyes briefly. "You didn't even try to use a spell or a stitch to get out of the stairwell?"

Mattie shrugged. "Like he said – it was only for a minute. We'd have gotten there eventually!"

Tillie tried her seer powers one more time. Nothing. "Mine still isn't working. Try yours."

Mattie held out her hands in front of her and they began to glow. "Mine works. Trevor?"

Trevor moved his fingers in a gesture and the door flew open. "Yep."

"So it's not the building – it's a spell on you," said Mattie. "That sucks. How do we lift it?"

"We can't without knowing who placed it. We'll have to make them release it," Tillie said. "Shezza, maybe?"

"Shezza's a stitcher," Trevor pointed out. "Has there been anyone else around you?"

"I was unconscious for a bit," said Tillie. "I think Shezza chloroformed me or something right after she stitched us out of the apartment. The next thing I remember was waking up in that cell. Oh! And then this very rude woman brought me some food and then took it away before I could eat it."

"That is rude," said Mattie.

"Did your magic work before she showed up?" asked Trevor.

"No," said Tillie. "That doesn't mean it wasn't her, though. She could have done it before, while I was out, and then left before I woke up."

"Did she talk to you?" said Trevor.

"A little."

"Try and remember the conversation," Trevor suggested. "Where did she live? Past, present, or future?"

Tillie struggled to recall the words the woman had used, but all she could remember was her name. She sighed. "I'm sorry, I don't remember. Even if Agent Poe was a speller, though, it doesn't mean she was the right speller."

"Agent Poe?" Mattie perked up and spun around, catching the door with one hand. "That's the Auditor who locked us in here!"

Tillie lifted her eyebrows in surprise. "I wonder how many Auditors there are in this building."

"I would imagine it's probably staffed up, right?" mused Mattie. "Getting ready for the big event."

Mattie's phone began to ring. "Giovani," she said. She answered it. "Hello? . . . Okay, okay! What's – Okay!" She hung up. "We gotta go."

"What happened?" demanded Trevor.

"I don't know. He sounded out of breath and just kept saying to get out now," she said.

Tillie's mind raced and she made a decision. "I'm staying. I'm going back in my cell and I'll be the woman on the inside. For real this time."

"You can't do that!" Mattie spun around again. "They're going to brainwash you!"

"It's a chance I'll take," Tillie said. "At least now we have some info on what's going on around here. Plus, we can't lose the chance to find out more about the court. This is probably our best chance to take these bastards down."

"Yeah, but—"

"And I can get out of my cell any time," Tillie reminded Mattie.

"But they don't know you can get out," said Trevor. "You're right. This is the best scenario."

"Oh, whose side are you on?" cried Mattie.

"Tillie's," he said. "I'm always on Tillie's side. Don't you remember?"

Tillie grinned at him. "And I'm always on yours, love." She popped up onto her toes to plant a kiss on his cheek. "See you guys later!"

Mattie held the door open for Tillie as she sauntered through. She walked back to her cell. Now all she had to do was figure out how the hell she was going to put the chain back on without magic.

14.

Mattie shook a finger at Trevor. "This isn't over, young man."

"I'm three months older than you," he pointed out.

"Irrelevant. Now let's get the fuck out of here."

She dashed back up the stairs and aimed a spell at the doors, unlocking and blasting them open without missing her stride. That may have been the most badass thing she'd ever done.

Mattie strode down the hall toward the exit, noting that it was a lot emptier than it had been before. In fact, there was not an Auditor to be seen.

"Does this seem off to you?" said Trevor.

"It does, actually," she replied. She paused and listened for sounds of – well, anything. There! Shouting off to the left. And then something that sounded like an explosion.

Mattie met Trevor's eyes.

"Do you think....?" he said.

"It's gotta be them! Come on!" Mattie turned down another hallway, heading toward the sounds.

The shouts and bangs began getting louder and louder and soon she could hear Ida's unmistakable voice yelling, "Take that, you sons of bitches! You'll think twice before kidnapping another Garaveldi, I suppose!"

Mattie and Trevor looked at each other and began to run. As she skidded around another corner, Mattie found herself in the middle of a fracas.

Actually, what she found herself in the middle of was a semi-circle of shields with a grim-faced group of Auditors on the other side and Giovani and Ida in the middle.

Giovani was calmly and systematically attacking the shields, searching for weak points with seer-white eyes and then aiming lightning at each point, so that the Auditors were scrambling to repair the shields. Only a couple of stitchers were attacking back, pulling books from another library room off to the left and winging them through the air to smack Ida and Giovani, each of whom had a small shield protecting their head and were completely ignoring any books that hit them anywhere else.

Ida was a sight to behold. Filled with fury, her shouts never ceased as she flung a steady stream of fireballs from one hand and what looked like daggers of pure energy with the other.

"What are you doing here?" asked Giovani, never skipping a beat in his shield attacks. "I told you to get out."

"We heard the commotion," said Trevor.

"Come on," said Mattie. "The way to the exit is clear. We'll cover you."

Giovani shook his head. "Auntie isn't exactly listening to reason right now. And I'm not leaving her."

"No problem." Mattie looked at Ida and extended a hand, placing a spell.

Ida levitated one inch above the ground. The old woman kept shouting and attacking, ignoring the fact that she was now floating away from the Auditors. "And you'll get your clutches on anyone else in my family over my dead body, you degenerate motherfucking brainwashed imbeciles," she screamed.

Mattie turned and strode back down the hall, setting the spell to drag Ida along with her.

"Come on," Trevor urged Giovani to follow.

Mattie broke into a run, her shoes pounding on the off-white tile floor. Ida's stream of insults finally wound itself down with, "And we'll be back and we're gonna shut you bastards down for good!"

"What did you tell them that for?" Mattie demanded, still running. "Now they'll be expecting us."

"Nah," said Ida. "I know how these kinds of organizations work. It's all rules and bureaucracy. It would take them weeks to figure out how to even start being ready for us, and by that time, they'll all be dead. I'd ask you to put me down, but I think we're going about three times as fast as I'd be able to on my own, so instead, I'll just thank you for the lift, I suppose."

"You're welcome," said Mattie, grinning. "But don't sell yourself short! You were giving those agents quite the run for their money back there!"

"Oh, sure. My magic's still as strong as ever. My knees, on the other hand...."

"Fair enough." Mattie crashed through the door to the outside and ran down the uneven sidewalk toward Trevor's car.

The car beeped as Trevor unlocked it with his fob.

Mattie opened the passenger door, lowered Ida gently to the ground, and then opened the back seat as Ida took shotgun.

Giovani slid into the seat beside her a split second later and Trevor into the driver's seat just after. He revved the engine as Auditors poured out of the building, crowding onto the sidewalk just outside the door.

Most were dressed as Mattie was used to seeing from the agents – skintight clothing, mostly leather, mostly brown or black, like movie assassins. But a few were wearing the most bizarre outfits she'd ever seen, colorful ensembles that fit oddly, more like the fashions you'd see on a runway, made to adorn a model in a show, but completely impractical for everyday life.

Mattie gave them the finger as they drove past and away. A couple of college students from the university just a couple blocks up watched curiously from their apartment balcony across the street.

In fact, all of the surrounding buildings were apartments, probably mostly hosting students. Mattie wondered idly what the residents thought took place in the building they'd just left. They probably assumed it was owned by the school, as most of the non-housing, non-bar buildings in this area were.

"So, what happened back there?" asked Trevor. "I thought we were being sneaky and just getting information."

"I got recognized," said Giovani. "I don't know what I was thinking – after all, I've been assigned to St. Louis half a dozen times, and the permanent staff here know me. Not to mention other field agents, but I guess

I thought field agents wouldn't know yet about my defecting. Apparently, station agents have been told."

"What's done is done. The question is, what next?" said Ida. She twisted around to peer into the back seat at her nephew. "We come back tomorrow with the cavalry? Shut the whole thing down? Come on, Giovani, you're the seer. Give us the plan!"

He shook his head, frustrated. "I don't know. I wish I knew exactly when the court was coming. We can't really take action until then."

"Tuesday," said Trevor. "Agent Poe said they'd be arriving on Tuesday."

Giovani sat straight up. "Poe, you say?"

"Do you know her?" asked Mattie.

"She locked us in a stairwell," said Trevor. "Although it's unclear why."

"Yeah," he said, softly. "I know Agent Poe. I wonder...."

"Tillie said Agent Poe was the one who brought her a tray of food, too," said Trevor. "But then took it back."

"Is that standard brainwashing procedure?" asked Mattie. "Bringing food and then taking it away before you can eat? To confuse you or something?"

"No," said Giovani. "Usually they bring you water while you're sleeping, but no food for at least a few days, and you don't see anyone at all."

"Why are they breaking protocol with Tillie?" Mattie wondered.

"Because Trevor was right," said Giovani. "It's not them. It's Poe. And she's on our side."

15.

Tillie settled down on one of the puffy bits on the floor, leaning against the puffy wall. All in all, it actually wasn't that bad in here. She wished she wasn't in her workout gear. She always felt better with a little bit of style.

If she could stitch, she would be able to pull something of her own from her closet at home, but that seemed pretty out of the question. She would also be able to use a stitch to close the chain on the door, as her efforts to do so with the shoelaces hadn't worked. She had fallen back on hoping that Poe would just think she'd forgotten.

Couldn't hurt to try, even if spelling and seeing didn't work. Maybe stitching miraculously would.

Tillie moved her fingers in a gesture of closing, picturing the chain on the door to her cell. She heard a small sound of metal on metal and sat upright. Had it worked? Had she actually stitched it? If so, that was the most complicated stitch she'd ever done – working with something she couldn't see and didn't belong to her. She felt the drain of energy that always came with stitching since it was the farthest from her own true nature.

And it meant the spell over her didn't cover stitches. That was crucial information.

She leaped to her feet and crossed the small room in a single bounce, wrenching open the door. It stopped, abruptly, caught on the chain. "Yes!" Tillie whirled around, outstretched arms brushing the walls of her tiny cell.

Now, for a change of togs. Tillie sat down again, crossing her legs in front of her, and thought for a moment. Her number one choice was always a dress or skirt, but that seemed impractical considering the circumstances. Jeans would probably be best and a simple long-sleeved top – it was a little bit chilly in this basement.

Tillie closed her eyes and pictured her dresser, mentally wiggling her way into the second drawer, where she kept shirts. Long-sleeved were on the right. She stitched with her fingers, grabbing whatever was on top.

Then she moved to the next drawer down and snatched up a pair of jeans. The final drawer contained undergarments, and she brought in a regular bra to replace the sports bra she was wearing.

She wavered on shoes for a moment – probably best to stick with the sneakers. And no, she really didn't need to bring along any jewelry.

She opened her eyes and smiled. There, in front of her, was a brand new outfit. She sagged against the wall, exhausted from her magical exertions. She made one more stitch and brought herself an organic protein shake from her fridge.

Opening the shake and taking a big gulp, she levered herself to her feet and changed her clothing, emptying the pockets of the cardigan and transferring her phone and a couple other odds and ends she had tucked away into the pockets of her jeans.

A moment of doubt pinged her. Would Agent Poe notice that her outfit had changed? She supposed that depended on whether Agent Poe was a stitcher. A speller or seer probably wouldn't.

Then again, she would need to send the old clothes back. Her captor might not notice that these were different clothes, but she sure would notice the pile of workout gear on the floor, and there was nowhere to hide them.

Tillie was already feeling more energized, whether from the positive change in clothing or the protein shake. She took a deep breath and stitched the yoga pants, cardigan, and sports bra back to her condo, dropping them on her bed and then falling back against the wall once again, almost completely drained.

She finished her shake, sent the empty bottle winging back to her kitchen, and then curled up to get some sleep.

16.

"Our side?" said Mattie. "Does this Poe person even know that there is an 'our side?'"

"I think you mean she's on whats-her-name's side," corrected Ida. "You know, the agent you killed and dressed up to look like Tillie."

"Agent Miller," supplied Trevor. "Right. Are Agent Miller's insurrectionists 'on our side,' exactly?"

"Well, they're also plotting to take down the organization, right?" said Giovani. "Doesn't that make them on our side?"

"No, they're plotting to take *over* the organization," Trevor corrected. "That's not the same thing."

"But what's the saying?" said Mattie. "Enemy of our enemies, right?"

"Bingo," said Giovani, pointing to Mattie. "That's what I'm saying."

"What it sounds like to me," said Ida. "Is that there are three sides and this splinter group of yours—"

"It's not my group," said Giovani. "I learned about it at the same time you did."

"Well, this splinter group of whoever's—"

"Agent Miller's," said Mattie.

"Can I just get a word in edgewise? Whatever happened to respect for your elders?" Ida snapped.

"Sorry."

"Thank you! The point I'm making is that this splinter group is its own side, but it's slightly closer to our side, so if we're all facing off against this court, then maybe we should ally with them. For now."

"And what happens after?" said Giovani.

"That's your department, I suppose," said Ida. "All I'm interested in is getting my great-nephew out of their clutches, and stopping them from kidnapping any more of my family. Or anyone else's family, I suppose. In fact, this whole shebang needs to be shut down. They've been preying on mages for long enough."

"Are the Splinters planning to continue the kidnappings after they take down the court?" asked Mattie.

"I would assume so," said Giovani. "They seem pretty dedicated to the cause of the organization, just not the leadership."

"So, we need to take down the Splinters, too," pointed out Trevor.

"One thing at a time, please," said Mattie. "First we take down the Auditors, then the Splinters."

"Is that their official name now?" Giovani raised an eyebrow. "They probably have one of their own, you know."

"Well, I don't know it, so I'm giving them my own," Mattie retorted.

"Can't we take them both down at the same time?" asked Ida. "Some of us aren't getting any younger."

"Wait a second," said Giovani. "Did you just say that Tillie told you that Agent Poe brought her a tray of food?"

Mattie frowned. "Yeah. So?"

"How do you know that? Did she call you again?"

"No, we ran into her," said Trevor.

There was a long, pregnant pause.

"So, where is she?" asked Ida, finally.

17.

Tillie woke up with a start. A key was scraping in the lock again. She sat up groggily as the door opened, rubbing her eyes and yawning. She felt like she'd only had a couple of minutes of rest.

Agent Poe entered. She was carrying another tray of food. Or maybe still carrying the same one. "Oh, good, you're awake."

"I wasn't until you showed up," said Tillie, a tad resentfully. "Are you going to leave that food this time?"

"Yes, actually. Things have changed," said Agent Poe. "We need to talk."

"Sure, as long as I can eat while we do so," agreed Tillie.

The Auditor sat down cross-legged and set the tray on the floor between them.

Tillie looked it over. It was very civilized, actually – ceramic dishes with tea, a couple of small sandwiches, and a scone with what was either chocolate chips or raisins. She hoped for chocolate chips.

Tillie poured a little milk into the tea and took a sip. She raised her eyebrows. "This is very good."

"Nothing but the best around here," said Agent Poe. She sneered slightly. "The court is coming, you know."

"Yes. Next Tuesday, right?"

Agent Poe froze. "What do you know about the court?"

A small smile played at Tillie's lips. "More than you'd think." She picked up one of the sandwiches and examined it. Cucumber and cream cheese. How cliché. She took a small bite and revised her opinion. Chevre, not cream cheese. And there seemed to be dill mixed in as well. Delicious.

Tillie glanced up at the Auditor again. She was watching her eat with narrowed eyes. Tillie took pity on the woman and set her sandwich down, swallowing her bite.

"Are we leveling with each other here? Forming an alliance? Let me guess – you're loyal to Agent Miller, not the organization."

The woman nodded, eyes still narrowed, arms crossed over her chest.

Tillie continued. "I want to take down the court as much as you do. Our end goals may be different, but it seems that our current goals may just be the same."

"Who are you, exactly?" asked Agent Poe. "How do you know so much? And why do you have a doppelganger running around here with someone who claims to be the Count of Prison Guards?"

Tillie choked mid-sip of tea. She cleared her throat. "The Count of Prison Guards?"

"It sounds ridiculous, I know," said Agent Poe. "But some of these courtiers have completely absurd titles. The only thing that clued me in that it wasn't on the level was the fact that the woman with him looked *exactly* like you, but with longer hair. And, of course, that the count wasn't dressed like a refugee from a Pride parade."

"That would be my identical twin sister, and the so-called Count of Prison Guards is my best friend." Tillie took another sip of the excellent tea, savoring it on her tongue before swallowing.

"And are you also connected somehow to the renegade Agent Garaveldi and the astonishingly powerful elderly speller who attacked a group of local station agents?"

Tillie set the teacup down, grinning hugely. "Ah, so you've encountered Auntie Ida, have you? Are you from St. Louis, by any chance?"

Poe shook her head. "A small town in Connecticut."

"So, you're not aware that the Garaveldi family is a prominent mage clan hereabouts, and Ida Garaveldi is its matriarch and basically unofficially rules the St. Louis mage community with a cheerful, but iron fist?"

"Um. No. I was not aware of that."

"Ah. Well, now you know." Tillie nibbled on the cucumber sandwiches as the rogue Auditor digested this information.

Poe cleared her throat and Tillie glanced up. The woman wore a thoughtful look. "Say we were to form an alliance." She paused.

"Yes?"

"Would said alliance include this Ida Garaveldi?"

"I'd like to see you try to keep her out."

"I think we'd very much like to have her on our side, actually. And what does your faction want, exactly?"

"Hmm. That's a tricky question." Tillie polished off the sandwiches and leaned back against the wall, teacup in hand. She took a sip as she thought about her response. It never paid to go into an alliance without at least some honesty. But she couldn't very well tell this woman that they wanted to dismantle the system that had essentially created who she was. "May I ask you one before I answer?"

"You can ask."

"Do you think I'm an abomination? Just because I sought to expand my horizons?"

Poe shrugged. Her lips pursed as she considered. "That's another tricky question, and one I've been working through for some time now. My conditioning says yes. That I was wrong to do so when I was younger and I need to make up for it by helping others learn the same lessons I did."

"But?"

"But the organization is corrupt in so many ways. Ever since I met Agent Miller, I've seen all of these little ways in which the core here is rotten. They're everywhere, once you start looking. Maybe we're – they're wrong about that too."

"Are you aware that members of the court are taught more than one discipline as children?" Tillie watched her captor closely.

Agent Poe's eyes widened. She was silent for a moment before she responded. "I guess that shouldn't surprise me. They're corrupt. That's the whole point."

Tillie studied the Auditor.

A whole gamut of emotions was making the rounds of the woman's face. She seemed confused, alarmed, thoughtful, and finally resigned.

Tillie made a decision, satisfied that Agent Poe was more willing to listen to reason than Shezza had been.

"Our goal is to take down the entire organization. Kill the court. Scatter the agents. Take Giovani's son and return him to the Garaveldi family."

"And the other children?" Agent Poe's eyes sharpened.

Tillie sucked in a breath. This one had a kid in the court too. She considered her answer very carefully. "None of us wants to kill any children."

"They travel with the main court," said Agent Poe. "What will you do with them?"

"We hadn't thought that far," Tillie admitted. "Ida is pretty focused on her nephew. If you join with us, you could have a say in our plans."

Agent Poe chewed on her bottom lip.

Tillie sipped her tea and waited.

Finally, Poe looked her straight in the eyes. "Do you know what happened to Agent Miller?"

Tillie was caught off-guard by the unexpected question and answered immediately. "We killed her."

Poe nodded. "I figured as much."

"Aren't you angry? The other agents who came after her seemed pretty pissed about it," said Tillie.

"It is what it is," said Poe. "She was assigned to bring you in, right? You were defending yourself. I can't blame you for that, especially at the same time that I'm considering how wrong we might be to be bringing in so-called abominations to begin with. It's a shame it was Miller, though. She was a good woman, a good agent, a good leader. Now that she's dead, I suppose I'm the de facto leader of our group." She took a deep breath in. "And I am cautiously prepared to negotiate with you and yours."

"Fair enough. Let me get them on the phone." Tillie pulled her cellphone out of her back pocket.

Poe's eyes widened. "You have your phone on you? How did you – wait a second! You were wearing yoga pants! That's why I assumed you didn't have any pockets and I didn't search you!"

Tillie smiled, sweetly. "Was I?"

"Yes. You were." Her eyes narrowed. "You stitched. You can stitch? Aren't you a seer?"

"Am I?" Tillie hit send, calling Trevor. She put the phone on speaker, so Poe could hear.

Mattie answered. "Tillie! What's going on?"

"Hey. I have a new friend here who wants to negotiate. Do we want to negotiate?"

"Who is your friend?" asked Giovani's voice.

Agent Poe leaned forward. "Hi, Garaveldi. It's Poe. I hear you've gone rogue."

"Yeah? I'm going to go out on a limb and suggest that maybe you have as well."

"Less rogue than you," she said. "Or at least smarter."

"Rogue enough to want to take these bitches down?" asked Mattie.

"Hell, yeah," said Poe, a vicious grin on her face. "Let's talk logistics."

Tillie took a bite of her scone. It was chocolate chip. This day kept getting better and better.

Half an hour later, Agent Poe and her tray of goodies were gone. Tillie's seer and spelling powers had been restored. She leaned back against the cushioned wall, her legs stretched out in front of her, and sighed.

She took a deep breath in and switched her sight into seer mode, exhaling with relief as it worked, just the way it was supposed to. The future was superimposed upon the present, nothing immediately in front of her, which made sense, since she was trapped in a tiny cell.

Tillie extended her seer power a little bit further, stretching it into the hallway and looking to see who would be coming and going for the next hour or so.

No one. Excellent.

She switched off her seer sight and scooted down so she was laying on the floor, her legs up on one pillowed spot and her head resting on another. It was actually pretty comfy. She stitched herself a blanket from her bed and snuggled in for a nap.

18.

Mattie paced her sister's living room, antsy and anxious. She hated this kind of thing – waiting until the optimal time to act. She wanted action and she wanted it now, dammit!

Trevor grabbed her hand as she passed him.

"What?" she snapped.

"You're distracting me. Sit down." He guided her toward a chair and she collapsed into it, huffily.

"Sit down and do what, exactly?" she demanded. "You're doing research. I'm no good at that. The Garaveldis are mobilizing their people. I wouldn't be any use there, because I'm not a damn Garaveldi. Tillie's probably doing something exciting back at Auditor HQ as a spy. What the hell am I supposed to be doing right now?"

"Waiting until—"

"No!" Mattie jumped to her feet once more and glared at him. "I can't just wait. Give me a fucking task or I will wear a rut on Tillie's beautiful floor."

"Make me a snack?" suggested Trevor. "Or you could practice spelling. I know you're getting pretty good, but you can always use more practice, right?"

"My shielding could use some work," she admitted. "Especially if we're going to be fighting some giant battle."

"Well, there you go." Trevor returned to his book, which was a treatise on the history of the court that he had stolen from the Auditors' library.

Mattie had no idea when or how he'd stolen it, but stolen it he had, and he was determined to study it. They had over a week until they could move against the court anyway.

Poe had told them that there would be an actual ball at the end of the week, like something out of fucking Cinderella, to welcome the court. They had decided that would be the best time to strike, while the court was gathered in one place.

That was going to be a long week, with very little for Mattie to do. She sighed and formed the words for her shield spell in her mind, picturing it as a solid wall.

A blurry force-field sprang up in front of her. Now what? She realized there was no way for her to test the shield against spells without any other mages to attack it. Well, stitchers tended to attack by moving objects around the room.

Mattie picked up a cushion and threw it at her shield. It collapsed.

Damn. She really did need a lot of work on her shields. Mattie put the shield back up, focusing on strength and solidity. She threw the pillow again.

Twenty minutes later, the shields were starting to hold up against cushionry and Mattie had switched to throwing small books.

Next up, large books.

After that, she cajoled Trevor into taking a study break and helping her out – stitching multiple books into her shield at unpredictable intervals.

"I'm getting pretty good at this," she grinned. "And I've only been practicing for –" she glanced at the clock on the wall. "Wow. Three hours."

Right on cue, her stomach rumbled.

Trevor laughed. He stood and stretched. "Shall we see what's in the fridge?

Mattie made a face. "Fancy shit. I want something I can sink my teeth into, not something to nibble on."

He picked up his phone. "There's a fantastic Thai place down the street that delivers here."

"Yes! I want pad see ew, please. Chicken and tofu. And potstickers, if they have them. And those little fried spring rolls. Fuck, I'm starving. Oh, and get peanut sauce for dipping the spring rolls in – they always come with that runny soy-sauce-based nonsense."

Trevor saluted. "Yes, ma'am! No runny nonsense allowed!"

As he made the call, Mattie wandered into the kitchen, grabbing a glass from the sleek, black cupboard and filling it with water from the graceful filter spigot next to the sink. She couldn't help but compare this modern kitchen with the vintage one from her old studio apartment in Portland.

She missed its retro charm – the tile countertops that were completely impractical and impossible to keep clean without special cleaners and plenty of elbow grease. The insanely shallow sink with its built-in drainboard that conveniently drained dishwater onto the black-and-white checkered floor on which half of the tiles were loose and used to come up when she swept.

But it was home. This wasn't home. It was a comfortable and beautiful space, and she knew it was exactly right for Tillie. But not for her.

She needed to figure out her next step. Would she go back to Portland? Probably not – she'd pretty much burned all of her bridges there. She would have to go back for her divorce hearing, whenever that was – next March, maybe? She made a note to look at her calendar.

Seattle was another option. It had been nice to reconnect with Cameron and he was going through a divorce of his own. Then again, maybe it was a little soon for both of them, and after all, there was a reason they had broken up back in college.

Mattie meandered over to the window and looked out over Washington Ave, a busy, trendy downtown street. This wasn't the spot for her, but maybe it was time to return to St. Louis for good, or at least for a while.

It was almost summer, so schools would be starting to look for new teachers as old ones retired or moved around to new jobs. Ida had hinted that she might be able to put in a good word at her old high school, which apparently had a vast alumnae network.

It was a Catholic school, but that might not be so bad. She'd tried public schools and had chafed at the rigidity of the rules. Maybe a private school wouldn't have to walk on so many eggshells.

She could rent a little brick house or apartment somewhere in south city. There was plenty of vintage charm to be had in St. Louis – more than in Portland. It was a city with an incredible amount of history. Trevor would help her look. His neighborhood had plenty of charm.

Mattie smiled at the realization that she'd made her decision and she strode into the living room to share it with Trevor. As she breathed in, she stopped abruptly and frowned.

"What's that smell?" she asked.

Trevor was just putting down his phone. "Food'll be here in an hour – I guess they're pretty busy today. What smell?" He breathed in deeply. "Oh, my god!"

Mattie and Trevor locked eyes and both realized at the same time. "Agent Parker!"

"I can't believe you forgot about him!" Mattie accused. "You're a stitcher! You're supposed to remember everything!"

"There has been a lot going on!" he protested. "What are we going to do with the body? We can't just leave him in Tillie's secret room!"

"Can we burn it?" Mattie suggested.

"Maybe. That's what we did with the other Auditors we killed," said Trevor. "But this time let's try not to burn down the whole building."

"They started that fire!" said Mattie.

"Fair enough. Sorry – I'm just trying to insert some levity into the situation!"

Mattie pointed to the fireplace. "Should we try to get him in there?"

Trevor rubbed his chin. "Yeah, that makes sense." He stitched and the body dropped onto the hearth. "Ugh. That smell!"

"What about his clothes and shoes and stuff?" said Mattie, trying to breathe as shallowly as possible. "Isn't it a lot of plastic? We shouldn't burn that."

"Right." Trevor stitched again and suddenly the corpse was naked.

"I feel like you could have left his underwear," Mattie muttered, averting her eyes. Not that she was a prude or anything, but she really didn't need to see some dead guy's ass.

"Next time be more specific, then," Trevor snapped. "I'm doing the best I can. Now what?"

Mattie murmured a spell. Her hands glowed and shot a fireball toward the fireplace. The corpse spectacularly failed to go up in flames.

"Um," said Trevor. "Can you make it hotter, maybe?"

"No, what we need is to build an actual fire, with tinder and kindling and everything," said Mattie. "Right? That's what we always did in Girl Scouts."

"I was never in Scouts," said Trevor. "I'm not much of an outdoorsy type."

"Right," said Mattie. "Well, what does Tillie use when she makes a fire in here?"

Trevor went over to the linen closet and pulled out a paper-wrapped cylinder with the words Eco-Log emblazoned on the side. "It's made out of old, dried coffee grounds or something," he said.

"We better use a couple of them," said Mattie. She held out her arms and Trevor tossed it to her.

He bent down and grabbed another one, placing it in the fireplace himself.

Mattie grabbed the wrought-iron poker and the coal shovel from their rack beside the hearth and gingerly poked the body to roll it further into the depths of the fireplace, careful not to pierce the skin. "What do you think is the best spot for the logs?"

"How would I know?" he asked.

"I don't know! Look it up!" She gestured to his phone on the table.

"Are you serious? That's a great way to get on an NSA watchlist!"

"Just use a thesaurus a bunch afterward and they'll assume you're a writer," Mattie suggested.

"I already use the thesaurus a lot," said Trevor.

"Then shut up and just look up how to burn a fucking body!"

"Fine." He scooped up his phone and typed furiously into the search engine.

Mattie waited, leaning against the poker and trying not to look at the fireplace. Her stomach rumbled again. How was she still hungry after all that? Thank goodness the Thai place was so busy, though – hopefully, they'd be done with this crap before the food came.

"The hair is the most flammable," said Trevor. "That makes sense – it's nice and dry."

"Yeah, the rest of this shit is way too squishy," said Mattie. She advanced on the fireplace again and pushed the logs toward the agent's head, lining them up end-to-end. "Okay, so we light the one under the head first and then the other one, so they're together and both burning and hope that the hair catches and then the rest of him?"

Trevor shrugged. "I guess so."

Mattie put the poker back on its rack and sent another fireball careening toward the logs. They both whooshed up in flames in a very satisfying way. She watched the hair closely. Strands were beginning to glow. "I think it's working!"

"Thank goodness," said Trevor. "What should I do with his clothes and stuff?"

"Where is it now?"

"I put it back in the secret room."

Mattie shrugged. "I guess just stitch it into the dumpster. Or no – a couple of dumpsters. Spread it out."

"Makes sense." Trevor made three stitching motions. "Done. Magic is pretty handy."

"I guess," said Mattie. "Life was easier before I knew it existed, though. Everything's so complicated now."

"Life is always complicated," said Trevor. "People have a tendency to look back and think things used to be simpler. But it's just that the complications change and when things get complicated in different ways it always feels like it's worse. You just have to learn to adapt with it."

Mattie raised an eyebrow. "Something you excel at."

He grinned. "It's always easy to give advice that you would never actually follow yourself."

Closing her eyes, Mattie sniffed the air and gagged. Her eyes snapped open and she stared into the fireplace, where the hair was now merrily burning and the back of the man's head was starting to turn brown. "Oh, god! The smell is getting worse."

Trevor's voice was muffled, as he clapped his hand over his mouth and nose. "Abort! Abort! Put the fire out!"

"Right!" Mattie flung a new spell at the flames, putting them out. She hastily erected an olfactory shield, breathing in relief as the stench cut off abruptly.

"Okay, new plan. Let's do the same thing with the body that you did with the clothes. Divide it up between dumpsters all across the city."

Trevor shook his head. "I can't stitch something into a place I've never seen. How many dumpsters do you think I've been to?"

Mattie stared at the body for a moment, thinking furiously. "What if we do it in really small pieces, so even if someone found several, they might not know what it was?"

"That could work."

Bracing herself for the smell, Mattie dropped the shield. She worked as quickly as she could, forming ten laser beams of energy that emanated from her fingertips and raking them over the corpse, cutting it into teeny pieces.

She tried not to think of them as bite-sized, but once the thought drifted into her mind, she couldn't seem to stop it. She focused on slicing it up smaller and smaller, until it no longer resembled a body, so much as a large pile of meat and sludge.

Mattie stepped back and put the smell shield back up, gagging and focusing very hard on not throwing up. "Okay, it's all yours." Her voice shook.

"I think this is good," said Trevor. His voice was faint too, although he seemed to be holding it together better than Mattie was. "Let's put it in some trash bags, and then I'll send the bags to a few different dumping spots."

"Sure." Mattie trotted into the kitchen and grabbed a box of green, compostable three-gallon garbage bags from under the sink. At least they wouldn't be adding to the plastic pollution.

Suddenly, her gorge rose and she couldn't hold it in any longer. Mattie lunged for the sink and vomited until all that was left was a sharp, acidic pain in her throat.

Her breathing shallow and ragged, she closed her eyes, leaning against the counter. She groped for the tap and ran water into the sink without opening her eyes. Then she felt around again and found the garbage disposal switch.

As the racket of the metal grinder filled the room, Mattie finally opened her eyes and used the sink sprayer to clear the sink of all evidence of her sickness.

Somehow, she felt calmer now.

She went back out to the living room, pausing in the doorway.

Trevor wasn't there.

She heard the sound of a toilet flush down the hall and realized that he'd been throwing up too. He'd picked a better spot for it.

Trevor walked into the room a minute later, looking calmer and less shaky himself. He strode back over to the fireplace and gave Mattie a small smile. "Better?"

"I think so." Mattie held up one of the green bags, shaking it out to expand it.

"Okay, you hold one open and I'll fill it up," Trevor instructed.

Mattie held the edges of the bag apart and watched as clumps of Agent Parker disappeared from the fireplace and appeared in the bag.

Once it was about half full, she said, "Okay, I think that's enough. These bags are kind of flimsy, and we don't want it to break."

"Fair enough." With one more twitch of his fingers, Trevor made the bag disappear.

Mattie sighed and opened another one. Her throat still ached. "Is this our life now?"

"I'm afraid so."

She nodded mournfully. "Just checking."

It took four bags to get all of the Auditor out of the condo, and with each bag, Mattie felt lower and lower. How had she managed to get to a point where she was getting rid of bodies?

And there would be more bodies. They were going into battle next week.

Maybe Scott had the right idea, refusing to participate. Could she plead pacifism herself? She wasn't a soldier. She was barely a mage. She was a high school English teacher.

Finally, Trevor sent the last bag of corpse bits straight to the landfill outside of town.

Mattie collapsed onto the couch, worn out.

Trevor sat down next to her. "I know," he said.

"What?" Mattie turned to look at him.

"I feel it too. This is surreal. A month ago, neither of us knew that magic existed. Neither of us had been involved in killing anyone. Neither of us would even have thought about killing anyone, except in a sort of jokey way. And now we're surrounded by people who seem to have no problem with it."

"They're so matter-of-fact about it," said Mattie.

"But you know what the worst part is?" said Trevor. "The worst part is that they're not new people. I've been living next to Ida for years. And Tillie — she and I have been best friends since we were eight."

"She's my twin sister," said Mattie, hollowly. "Since you were eight? We were literally in the womb together."

"I know," said Trevor again. His phone dinged and he pulled it out of his pocket. "The food's here."

"I'm not hungry anymore," said Mattie.

19.

Tillie yawned and stretched. Then she frowned. Something had woken her up. What was it? She glanced at her phone. She'd slept for longer than she'd meant to.

Her feeling of unease grew and she switched into seer sight, looking out into the hallway. Someone was coming and it wasn't Agent Poe. She watched as the person checked each cell, starting at the other end of the hall.

She only had a couple of minutes before they showed up. Could she stitch herself out? Definitely not – that was way beyond her abilities. Tillie switched off her seer sight and pushed herself into a corner of the room, concentrating on staying very still. She waited for the knob of her cell to twist and then she began to murmur, as quietly as she could, a spell to blend in with her surroundings.

As a nondescript woman with lank blonde hair glanced around the room, Tillie held herself completely still except for her lips, which moved automatically in a constant loop of her camouflage spell.

The woman closed the door again and moved on to the next room.

Tillie remained still for another moment. Agent Poe hadn't said anything about regular sweeps of the cells. Surely, if she'd been expecting that, she would have warned Tillie. So, either Poe wasn't as well-informed as she thought she was, or something unusual was going on.

This called for some reconnaissance of her own.

Tillie checked her pockets to make sure she had everything she might need and ran through the inventory of her shoes again too. Then she switched back into seer mode and checked the hallway again. The woman had apparently finished her cell check and moved on.

She slipped out into the hallway, heading in the opposite direction of the stairwell she'd found Mattie and Trevor in last time.

She felt a lot better about exploring now that she had her mage abilities. She left her seer sight on so she could avoid anyone else moving around the building. At the end of the hall was another corridor. She picked a direction at random and walked down the passage. It was lined with doors and she could see that they were all empty of people.

Unfortunately, that's all she could see – she wished, not for the first time, that seers could see objects through walls rather than just sensing people and their actions. Immediately, she felt guilty – getting greedy about wanting more power was what had gotten her into this mess.

Then again, that was Auditor thinking, right? Stay in your own place and don't deviate from your own discipline? Tillie's lips tightened. No outdated secret society was going to tell her what to do. Maybe there was a way to see through walls. After all, she could see distant places through scrying. Maybe she could combine stitching and seeing or something.

She should ask Giovani if he'd ever tried it. In the meantime, she would have to open the doors to look into the rooms.

Tillie reached for the handle of the nearest room, but it refused to turn. She pulled out her lockpick set and got to work.

Half an hour and three rooms later, Tillie was bored out of her mind. You'd think the clandestine headquarters of a secret society would be more interesting. Instead, it was room after room filled with boring books about boring shit and meeting rooms with tables and coffee bars. It was like being in a university humanities building.

Probably. She hadn't gone to a university, so she was just guessing there. But it seemed like the kind of place Trevor would have been excited about, and not in a good way. Much as she loved Trevor, he was definitely a nerd.

She slipped out of a room lined with books on the history of magery, most of which seemed to be treatises on how no one in the history of magery had successfully used multiple disciplines. These guys seriously took all of the fun out of magic.

She glanced toward the next room with her seer sight and grinned. Finally! Some action! This room had people in it - and one of them was Agent Poe. Tillie returned to the duller-than-rocks history room and strode toward the back of the room, where there was a mottled green countertop with a sink sunk into it.

Beside the sink was a row of the kind of plain white mugs you'd expect to see in a diner and some coffee-making implements.

Tillie grabbed a white ceramic sugar bowl, dumped its contents into a plastic trash can under the counter, and filled it with water. She seated herself at the nearest table and peered deep into the dish, concentrating on forming the image of Agent Poe.

The picture began to rise from the bottom of the bowl and a voice filled the air. Tillie smiled in satisfaction. Not every seer could scry with audio too. She zoomed out so that she could see the whole meeting, not just Poe. There were three other agents with her and they seemed to be arguing.

"Look, I don't trust her!" A man with light brown skin and a pinched look to his face smacked his hand down on the table in front of him as he directed his ire toward Poe. "And I don't get why you do!"

"She killed Miller," pointed out another woman who was dressed all in black vinyl like a character from a 90s cyberpunk movie.

Tillie grinned. How did someone dressed like that expect to be taken seriously?

But no one else was amused. The other two strangers were nodding emphatically and Poe had her hands raised in a gesture of placation.

"I see where—"

"I don't think you do!" shouted Pinch Face.

Poe frowned and her hands glowed.

Pinch Face tried to continue speaking, but no sound emerged. He subsided, resentment smoldering in his deep brown eyes.

"Anyone else?" Poe looked around and lowered her hands. Their glow receded. "I understand. Agent Miller was an important part of this movement. But think back. I know it's hard to do but try. Think back to before you were an agent. When you were a young mage, trying to expand your horizons."

Tillie blinked, startled to hear her own words echoed.

"It's hard to remember," said Cyberpunk slowly.

"I know," said Agent Poe. "It's like remembering a movie you saw, right? Or a story that someone else told you."

Cyberpunk nodded.

"Doesn't that seem odd?" Poe persisted. "Don't you think it's messed up that we can remember so vividly our lives in the organization, but the time before seems fuzzy?"

"We've been brainwashed," said Pinch Face.

"Exactly," said Agent Poe. "Doesn't that make you angry?"

"Of course it does!" Cyberpunk pounded a fist on the table in front of her. "But—"

"Just think back, as best you can," Agent Poe interrupted. "Did any of you have advanced warning that they were coming?"

The assembled mages shook their heads.

"I did. A seer friend saw a vision and told me. I tried to run, just like this Holiday woman did. And I tried to fight back. Can you blame me?"

"You were an abomination," muttered Cyberpunk.

"That's your conditioning talking," Poe retorted sharply. "Can't you see that? It's your conditioning that blames Tillie for defending herself."

"Yes, of course we see that," said the third listener, quietly. He was a thoughtful-looking man, dressed in a plain black t-shirt and well-tailored jeans. He reminded Tillie a little bit of Trevor, but white, with a smattering of freckles and dark brown hair. "It's one thing to see it and another to overcome it."

Agent Poe bowed her head in respectful acknowledgment of his point. "Fair enough. Thank you for that insight, Agent Thomas."

Agent Thomas smiled slightly. "Maybe it would help if we began to reclaim our first names. You may call me Aaron if you'd like."

There was a pause as all three of the other Auditors looked slightly shocked. Poe recovered first and placed a hand on her heart. "You do me a great honor. Aaron. My name is Nicole."

Pinch Face stood and placed his hand on his own heart. He took in a deep breath and exhaled heavily. "I am Matthew. I used to go by Matt when I was a kid."

"Nice to meet you," said Nicole. "Which would you prefer we call you?"

He paused. "I think Matthew. I'll reclaim it, but still acknowledge that I am a new person. Matt just sounds so carefree. I am no longer carefree."

Cyberpunk stood as well. "Hello, Matthew. Nicole. Aaron. My name is Danielle."

Tillie brushed her cheek with her fingers and was astonished to find that she was crying. Well, why not? This was a big moment for these people. And that could have been her. She wasn't so vain as to think she would have been immune to brainwashing.

If not for Giovanni, she would have been caught and conditioned just like them.

She studied Aaron's face. This one bore watching. He had diffused a situation that had seemed sure to end in violence. He had remained silent until the right moment and then spoken quietly and evenly. The man had charisma and restraint, a rare combination.

Tillie shivered. She was glad he was on her side.

20.

The next morning, Mattie woke up with a jolt. Something was wrong. She rubbed her eyes, threw back the covers, and rolled out of Tillie's guest bed.

BANG BANG BANG. That's what had woken her. Someone was pounding on the door to the condo.

Mattie yawned and made her sleepy way down the hallway, through the living room, to the entrance. She opened it and blinked at Giovani.

"What time is it?" she asked, still groggy.

"I know, I'm sorry." He pushed his way past her and stood in the middle of the room, tugging at his sandy hair.

Mattie closed the door and leaned back against it, studying him. His eyes looked slightly bloodshot and sunken, with dark bags underneath. His chin was covered in a sandy stubble and his usually smooth hair was askew, as though he'd been fidgeting with it.

His shoulders hunched uncertainly as he stood there, watching her in turn.

"You look like shit, dude," she said, finally.

Giovani nodded rapidly. "Yeah, I'm freaking out."

"Is something wrong with the plan?" said Mattie.

"No! No, the plan is great. Going smoothly. All good there." Giovani sighed and turned away, shakily walking over to the couch and sitting down. He leaned back and closed his eyes. "My life, on the other hand. . . ."

"Sure." Mattie made her way to the chair opposite him. "I guess I've been so focused on the Auditors, I hadn't thought about what you're going through."

"Until a couple of weeks ago, my life was dedicated to an organization that I'm now plotting to overthrow," said Giovani. He opened his eyes and sat up. "I'm staying with my father, who I haven't seen in fifteen years, and who is clearly trying really hard to bury a deep resentment toward me for being kidnapped and brainwashed—"

"I'm sure that's not—"

"No, I know it's not exactly that." Giovani scrubbed his face with his hands. "But it's hard for me not to feel like I'm being blamed for something that happened to me. I guess I'm partly to blame, but—"

"Nope." Mattie put a ton of steel into her voice. "Shut that down."

Giovani stared at her. "What?"

"That victim-shaming bullshit. Shut it down. You are not to blame for being kidnapped and brainwashed. That is not your fault. You didn't break any laws. You didn't do anything wrong except from the point of view of those bastards who kidnapped you. That is one hundred percent on them."

"Yeah, but—"

"Nope."

"Okay, but—"

"Nope."

A faint smile formed on Giovani's face. "Nope?"

Mattie grinned. "Damn straight. I know logic doesn't always come into feelings. I know it's easier to blame yourself. But keep practicing blaming the people actually responsible, and it'll get easier."

"Thanks." Giovani ran a hand over his already-disheveled hair. "I'll do my best."

"What else?" said Mattie. "It's not just your dad that's got you in this state."

He sighed again. "I'm essentially re-entering the real world right now. For the past fifteen years, the only non-Auditors I've spoken to have been food service workers and people I was trying to kidnap."

"Seriously?" Mattie stared at him. "It's that contained?"

"We stayed in HQs and safe houses. Maybe an occasional motel if we were really out in the middle of nowhere, but even then, you'd just get your key from the front desk and that was it. We drove cars that the organization provided. We saw doctors who were retired agents – honestly, I have my doubts now that they were actually doctors and not just marginally-trained medics. We had everything provided to us. The only time I would talk to someone outside the organization was when I was on the road and I'd stop for meals."

"Wow. So, basically, your life has been turned completely upside-down, and instead of giving you time to process it, we're asking you to stage an elaborate coup against the very people you were fighting for less than a month ago."

Giovani shook his head. "No one's asking me to. I believe in this. And honestly, I think the distraction is doing me good. It's just that the need to pretend that

I'm a totally put-together, on-top-of-it, super-competent leader is wearing me down."

"Got it. So you came here because you knew that I was the last one equipped to judge anyone for being a complete mess."

He shrugged. "In a nutshell. And I thought maybe you could use some help sparring and that would distract me some more."

"Yes. Absolutely. I have got your back on both those counts." Mattie grinned and stood. "How about some breakfast first and then sparring?"

Giovani's answering smile took about ten years off his face. "Yes to that."

21.

Tillie woke up to her phone's alarm. She'd been sleeping in her workout gear, so she got straight into her morning exercise, working out around the odd, pillowy bumps in the floor. Probably good practice for an actual battle – her previous experiences had only been fighting one or two people at a time. The upcoming coup would be utter chaos and she'd have to deal with distractions, so an oddly bumpy floor was helpful.

As she moved through her forms, she went over today's agenda in her head. She had a full day coming up of strategy meetings, pep talks, recruitment, and possibly even some group magic workings.

No rest for the revolutionaries.

22.

"Can I ask you a question?" said Giovani. He erected a hasty shield just as Mattie lobbed a fireball spell at him. It fizzled out on the marble floor of Tillie's hidden ritual room.

"Just ask. I hate it when people ask if they can ask. If I don't want you to ask it, I just won't answer." Mattie deflected Giovani's lightning and then threw another ball of flame, shifting her own shield to the side just long enough to do so and then moving it back into place.

"Your name is Mattie." He threw a curved blast of energy around her shield and she extended it just in time.

"Tricky, tricky," she said.

"The enemy will be all around you in the actual battle," Giovani admonished. "You can't rely on a shield that only covers one side of you."

"Fair enough." Mattie focused and extended her shield into a cylinder that surrounded her. "Is that your question? Telling me my name?"

"And your sister's name is Tillie."

"Again, not a question." Mattie tossed a fireball straight up into the air and then pushed it toward

Giovani before it could drop down onto her. He deflected it easily.

"Your shield should cover your head too," he said. "Your enemy will catch onto that trick pretty quickly. All I'm saying is that Mattie and Tillie are both short for Mathilda."

"Impressive." Mattie grinned. "Most people don't catch onto that." She dropped her shields briefly to throw another fireball, focusing on immediately putting the shields back up.

"That's better," said Giovani. "But have you considered combining your spelling with stitching so that you can keep your shields in place?"

Mattie frowned. "What do you mean?"

"Create the fireball with a spell. But instead of throwing it with a spell, stitch it to the other side of your shields and then throw it."

"If I can do that, can't I just stitch it right to them?"

"No, you can only breach your own shields with a stitch, not your opponent's. And stitchers and seers may team up with spellers, so be prepared for everyone to have shields," said Giovani. "So, how exactly do twins end up with the same name?"

"Oh, it's your classic tale of new-mom-on-drugs," said Mattie. "They didn't know they were having twins. Somehow it never showed up on the ultrasound. So they only picked out one name. " She made a fireball and then paused, concentrating hard on moving her fingers exactly how Trevor had taught her to move an object across a room. The shield stopped it, and the fireball just hovered in the air. Her energy levels dropped abruptly. "What am I doing wrong?"

"Don't try to move it through the room with your stitch," said Giovani. "You could do that with a spell and not drain your energy so quickly. You create a portal for it and make it blink out where it is and then place it where you want it with another portal."

"Right." Mattie moved her fingers again and then the fireball slammed into Giovani's shields.

"Good! Do it again!"

Mattie did it again. And again. "Anyway," she said as she continued practicing, "we were born early and Dad was out of town. Mom was by herself and a bit loopy and when they asked what our names were, she said Mathilda. And then they asked about the other one, and she just kept saying Mathilda, and here we are."

Giovani laughed. "And no one ever corrected the situation?"

Mattie shrugged, sending another fireball directly into Giovani's shields. "I don't know if they couldn't change it after the fact or if they could but they didn't know how or if they decided it was fine. I just know that they called me Mattie and Tillie Tillie and it's been a pain in my ass my whole life." She dropped her own shields and stumbled toward one of the couches that had been pushed aside. "I gotta stop. This is too much stitching for me."

Giovani walked over to sit beside her, stitching in a bottle of water as he did so. He handed her the water. "It'll get easier. You just have to practice."

"I don't know if I can practice enough by Friday to make it worth doing in battle," said Mattie.

"That's okay." He stitched in another water and drained it. "Practicing stitching will still build your spelling stamina. Like athletes training with extra weight. And then you'll have the skills if you need them on the day."

Mattie finished off her own water and set it down on a small end table. "Okay, let's get back to it, then."

23.

Tillie sat quietly in the back of the room as Agent Poe – Nicole – addressed a group of fifteen Auditor agents-turned-rogue.

"And so we've concluded that the only ethical thing to do is to completely dismantle the organization from the inside," said Nicole. "The opportunity to overthrow the court has been handed to us with the upcoming occupation here in St. Louis. We have the advantage of our group's leadership right here at HQ. And now we have new allies from the outside world."

A murmur ran through the crowd.

Nicole beckoned to Tillie and she strode up to join her at the front of the room, feeling like she was back in high school, coming up to give a book report or something.

Nervously, she cleared her throat. "Hi. I'm Tillie Holiday, and I was almost one of you."

She glanced around the group, her eyes meeting Aaron's. He gave her an encouraging nod and she smiled slightly, taking heart.

"I am here as a representative of a group of people who recently learned of the Auditors and who share your mission of taking them down."

A tall, thin woman in the front row interjected. "This is the first I've heard of taking the whole organization down. Where did this idea come from?"

"It's not a new idea," said Nicole. "Agent Miller and I talked about it on multiple occasions. She was beginning to think that the organization as a whole was doing wrong. We argued over it. My wish now is to carry on the mission she truly believed in, going beyond simply rebelling against the court."

Tillie raised an eyebrow, wondering if that was true. If so, it was the first time Nicole had mentioned it. If not, then she was a true politician and someone to keep a stern eye on. Aloud, however, she only said, "New information has also come to light regarding the court's hypocrisy." She recounted what Giovani had said about his son.

Nicole added, "After hearing this, I also contacted my daughter, who is fourteen and being educated by the court, and she confirmed that she is being taught to morph."

Another murmur ran through the crowd, this one angry. The woman who had spoken before stood up. "I'm in."

One by one, the attendant rebels rose and gave their approval.

24.

On Sunday morning, Mattie opened the door to find Giovani with a tray of breakfast sandwiches and cardboard coffee cups.

"Back for more sparring and venting?" she said, stepping aside to let him in.

"I brought gifts this time," he said with a grin. "Chai latte, right?"

"Aw, you remembered!" Mattie grabbed the proffered cup and snagged a sandwich too, unwrapping it and taking a big bite.

She eyed the former Auditor while she chewed. He had shaved today and brushed his hair, and he looked like he'd actually gotten some sleep too.

"Yesterday really helped," said Giovani.

"You should really be seeing an actual therapist, you know," said Mattie. "I'm not super qualified to help you work through the very real trauma you've suffered."

Giovani nodded. "Yeah, I know. But it's hard to do that when you have no insurance, no job, not even a valid driver's license."

"Wow, yeah. I never even thought about all that." Mattie took another bite, chewing thoughtfully. "What kind of work did you do before?"

He shrugged, sipping his coffee. "Nothing. I was in college. I had a work-study job in the accounts payable department at school. Just doing filing."

Mattie sipped her chai, which was excellent. "What were you studying?"

"Communications."

"Ah." She nodded sagely. "The major for people who don't know what they want to do, but have been told by their advisor to pick a major."

"Bingo."

"Well, you have a blank slate now. You can do anything you want. Your life has been returned to you."

Giovani raked his hands through his hair, completely destroying the put-together look he'd so clearly been cultivating. "I know, and it stresses me out!"

"Why?" Mattie cocked her head.

"Because I have no idea what I want to do! I've never known. The only time in my life I've ever had a purpose was when I was with the Auditors!" He jumped to his feet and started pacing.

Mattie grabbed his arm as he passed and pulled him back down beside her. "Dude, you are gonna drive me crazy with all of that pacing. Look. You don't have to have a grand purpose. And you don't have to figure it out right now. After all, right now your purpose can be destroying the Auditors, right?"

He nodded and exhaled deeply. "Right. Right. That's a purpose."

"And you can worry about a job later."

"Sure."

She drained the last of her chai and wadded up the wrapper from her breakfast sandwich, tossing it on the coffee table. "What you need right now is action and distraction. Let's spar."

25.

Tillie rubbed her temples. The problem with fomenting a rebellion was that you couldn't just gather everyone in one room and give a single speech. It had to be done stealthily. From what she'd gathered, Agent Miller had been great at this.

There were agents all across the country who were involved in the uprising. Everywhere she'd gone, Agent Miller had approached Auditor agents on the road, in HQs, in safe houses, and talked them into joining up.

Then she'd manipulate the system to get those agents sent to St. Louis HQ, where Agent Poe, her second-in-command was stationed. Nicole would cement their loyalties and keep them in the loop, even once they got sent back out into the field.

As a result, almost every agent in this HQ was part of the revolution and dedicated to following Nicole's orders.

They were less enthused about Tillie taking over as Nicole's second-in-command now that Agent Miller was dead. Especially when they learned what had actually happened to Agent Miller.

And to add to the stress, there were still a handful of agents on site who either hadn't been approached or, worse, had been felt out and declined to join up. So those agents needed to be avoided at all costs.

To say nothing of the handful of courtiers who really had been sent in ahead to get ready for the main event.

Nicole was working on getting the agents who were loyal to the court traded out and more rebels sent in to replace them. Tillie wasn't really sure how that worked, but she figured it was above her paygrade. What she needed to focus on was getting these Auditors to accept that after the battle they would no longer be Auditors.

To that end, she, Nicole, and Aaron were meeting individually with those agents who seemed most intractable.

"This seems very drastic," said Agent Jameson. "Very all-or-nothing."

"I disagree," said Tillie. "What I think seems drastic is maintaining a cult for hundreds of years. That's what this so-called 'organization' is. The court holds its dominance by only allowing people born into the group to have any kind of power and then creates a self-expanding congregation by instructing its members to kidnap and brainwash outsiders who break an arbitrary rule."

"The rule isn't arbitrary," Jameson objected.

"That's true," said Aaron. "It's a rule that keeps mages in check. A rule that prevents those outside the organization from gaining power that the court itself is tapping into."

Jameson's mouth opened and closed a couple of times like a koi waiting to be fed. "They're tapping into what, exactly?" she said, finally.

"The court trains its own to use multiple disciplines," said Tillie, wearily, for about the twelfth time that day. She glanced at the clock on the wall. It was only noon. "They call it morphing."

Jameson looked to Aaron and Nicole for confirmation. Nicole nodded. "It's true. They've been doing it for centuries, and the universe has yet to implode."

"That we're aware of," said Aaron with a gentle smile.

Jameson bared her teeth in a ferocious grin. "Okay, I'm in. What do you need from me?"

Nicole briskly consulted a page in front of her. "You'll be in Group 3. Report to Danielle Beck in Meeting Room 12 tomorrow morning at 8:00."

Agent Jameson blinked. "Danielle?"

"We've begun reclaiming our first names. The first step in reclaiming our own lives," said Aaron. "Would you feel comfortable sharing yours?"

The agent was speechless for a moment.

"I'm Nicole," said Nicole. "This is Aaron."

"Erica," said Agent Jameson. "My name is Erica." A single tear rolled down her cheek.

26.

Mattie's breathing was growing uneven and heavy as she dodged attacks by Giovani, Trevor, and Ida all at the same time. Her shields were beginning to weaken and she desperately reached for the last of her inner reserves, pushing the shields outward to physically shove her attackers off-balance.

Giovani stumbled backward into Trevor, and Mattie threw a paralysis spell at them both while they were distracted. Then she grabbed Ida by the arm and held her in front of herself as a human shield.

"Enough!" she gasped. "I need a break!"

"Nice work," Ida praised her. "You're getting much better in a really short time."

"I mean, what other choice do I have?" Mattie panted. "I get good or I die, right?"

"Fair enough," said Ida. "Learning is situational, I always say."

Mattie released Giovani and Trevor from the spell holding them in place.

"Do you really always say that, Ida?" Trevor teased.

"I think I've said it once or twice." Her black eyes danced. "Come along, then, and let's have a rest. Then it's your turn, young man."

Trevor nodded, bleakly. "I'll be glad to get some practice in. I have a terrible feeling I'm going to die on Friday."

"What a thing to say!" said Ida. She led the way through the secret door into Tillie's living room. "How about some tea?"

"I'll help," said Mattie, following Ida into the kitchen.

"How about you, dear?" said Ida. She picked up the kettle and paused, giving Mattie a piercing look. "Are you afraid you'll die on Friday?"

Mattie shook her head. "I know I might. But that's not what's really bothering me about the battle."

"You're afraid you'll kill," Ida observed. "I know that look. The conscience-stricken look of someone who hasn't done anything wrong yet but is terrified to know that it's coming."

Mattie nodded, grateful that she hadn't been forced to put her fears into words. "I'm not a killer, Ida. I'm an English teacher."

Ida strode to the sink to fill the kettle with water. "You can't be both?"

"It doesn't feel like I *should* do both," said Mattie.

"Why is that, dear?"

"My life isn't worth more than someone else's!" Mattie sighed and threw herself onto a stool at the breakfast bar. "What gives me the right to go into these peoples' home and start slaughtering them?"

"What gave them the right to come into Giovani's home and take him to their training facilities and turn him into a killer?" Ida countered. "What gave them the right to try to do the same to Tillie?"

"But the people who did those things were also victims," said Mattie. "That's what really bothers me about this whole thing. If I could go back in time and kill the people who started the Auditors, before they could get the whole thing off the ground, that would be one thing. But the agents, they're just brainwashed kidnapping victims, right?"

Ida leaned against the counter, her head cocked. "Well, luckily it sounds like Tillie and her friends are ensuring we won't have to face any agents on Friday. So you must be concerned about killing members of the court too. Why them?"

"Born into that life. Again, not something they chose."

"These are excellent points," said Ida. "Points that have been made over and over again by pacifists everywhere. And yet, we continue to fight each other."

"Why?" asked Mattie. She slumped in her seat. "What good will it do?"

"Is that a general question or one specific to us going in this Friday and wiping out the Auditors' court?"

"I don't know. Both, I guess."

"Well, I'll answer the specific one first, then, I suppose." Ida sat down on the stool beside Mattie's, resting a hand on her shoulder. "It's going to break a harmful cycle, and it's going to do it quickly. Believe it or not, by attacking this HQ and exterminating the court, we'll be saving a ton of lives. We'll take some lives, lives that have not been terribly innocent, and save lives of people who are, by and large, innocent."

"But it's not their fault they were born into the court," repeated Mattie.

Ida nodded, thoughtfully. "Tell me, dear, do you like termites?"

Mattie raised an eyebrow. "I feel like that's the kind of question you don't really need me to answer, but you're going to use it to make a point."

"You're too smart for your own good, dear," said Ida. "So, let's just assume you don't like termites, then, I suppose."

"Accurate."

"How about kittens? Do you like kittens?"

"Of course."

"Now," said Ida, "if you found a building that was infested with kittens, what would you do?"

Mattie grinned. "Take a million pictures and then call an animal shelter."

"You'd rescue them, in other words. And if you found a building infested with termites?"

"I guess I'd do my best to kill them," said Mattie.

"But it's not their fault that they were born termites instead of kittens, is it?" Ida gave her a smug look. "But you'd exterminate them because you know that if you didn't, they'd keep multiplying and doing a great deal of harm."

"Yeah, okay," said Mattie.

Ida slid her arm around Mattie's shoulder. "I'm going to tell you a secret, dear. I hate killing. I hate battle and wars and combat of any kind. But I've been a warrior all my life."

Mattie leaned into the hug. "You're such a badass, Ida."

"I suppose that's one way to put it. But that wasn't the secret. The secret is that I would never go into battle with anyone who wanted to kill. I will only fight on the side of people like you."

The kettle began to sing, and Mattie reluctantly pulled away from Ida, going to pull it off the flame of the gas stove. She peered into the infuser that sat next to the teapot on the counter. "You forgot to put tea leaves in here, Ida."

"Silly me. I got distracted, I suppose. Well, it's afternoon, so better make it green. I can't handle too much caffeine in one day at my age."

Mattie nodded and spooned two tablespoons of green tea leaves into the infuser. "Do you think we'll ever stop fighting?"

"Nope," said Ida. "I think war is part of the balance of life. I think there will always be greedy bastards who try to take all of the power, and there will always be warriors like you and me who see them do it and stand up and say, 'Stop that.' And then when the greedy bastards refuse to stop it, we kill them."

Mattie smiled. "It sounds so simple the way you say it."

"Well. I've done a lot of thinking about it, I suppose. I've lived a long time. And I'm still fighting."

Her smile widened. "I want to be you when I grow up, Ida."

27.

Tuesday came at last, and Mattie and Trevor were positioned down the street from the Auditor HQ, waiting for the court to arrive. Co-conspirators were positioned on the other three sides of the building.

Giovani wanted to make sure nothing unusual happened. There was always the chance that a seer among the court would have had a vision, which was another reason they were waiting until Friday to make their move.

Tillie and her rogue agents had spent the past few days putting dampening spells all over the building so that no one could have any visions. It wouldn't affect regular seer sight – only prevent spontaneous prescience, so the court shouldn't get suspicious about it.

"What time is it?" asked Mattie again.

"I swear, you're worse than a five-year-old on a road trip," Trevor groaned. "You have your own phone. You can check for yourself."

"Sorry." She drummed her fingers on the dashboard, not bothering to check the time. It didn't really matter. What she really needed was a distraction. But that would defeat the purpose of being on watch.

Another car drove past and she snapped her head around to watch it.

"That's not them," said Trevor. How did he stay so calm? "They'll be in a bus."

"A bunch of busses, I know," said Mattie. "The fancy tour-type busses."

"But probably only one or two to each door," Trevor reminded her.

"Right, right." She restrained herself from asking for the time again. There wasn't a set time that the court was supposed to start arriving. Just sometime between noon and four. It was like waiting for someone to come and fix the internet.

And then suddenly, there it was. A huge, sleek silver-and-black bus, like something a major rock star took on tour. It was the bus equivalent of a billionaire's yacht, and it inched its way down the narrow city street.

"It's like it's defying physics," Trevor murmured, awe in his voice. "Half the time I feel like I'm barely getting my Subaru down these roads."

"Look." Mattie pointed at the cars parked on either side, just ahead of the bus.

"Someone's stitching them out of the way," Trevor observed.

Sure enough, as the bus crawled forward, cars were jumping right up to the curb to make more space for it.

"So, it's definitely them," said Mattie. "And not, say, SLU's girls' basketball team, back from an away game."

"Like a girls' team would ever warrant that kind of equipment," snorted Trevor. "College athletics are way too sexist for that."

Mattie didn't respond, just watched wide-eyed as the coach finally stopped directly in front of the door to the Auditor's headquarters. She finally pulled out her phone and sent off a quick text to Giovani, letting him know they had eyes on the court.

Giovani responded immediately.

"The western door has one too," Mattie relayed. Another text came in. "And now the south door as well."

"Two down," said Trevor. "Six to go."

"I can't decide if it's better now that it's starting or worse," Mattie groaned. "Now I've got the adrenaline of 'Oooh, something's happening,' but the reality is that I can't actually *do* anything about it for three more days."

"They're starting to disembark," said Trevor. His voice was breathless.

Mattie craned her neck for her first glimpse of the court. It wasn't every day that you got to see royalty, even if they were the royalty of an obscure secret society and not an actual country.

"Oh, wow," she breathed. She'd thought the agents dressed a bit eccentrically. They had nothing on these people.

The first person to disembark was a woman with spiky purple hair. Not short spiky purple hair, but huge, two-foot spikes of hair, each spike a different shade of purple, ranging from a lavender so light as to be almost silver to a deep almost-black.

The woman was dressed in a green-and-black corset top that left very little of her bosom to the imagination and cinched in her waist in a way that could not be healthy. Paired with this was a long cream-colored skirt with—

"Is that a bustle?" said Trevor.

"She's like if a renaissance fair threw up on a punk rocker," said Mattie.

"Oh, my god, here comes another one," said Trevor.

This one was a person of indeterminate gender with platinum hair piled on top of their head in a huge beehive. They were dressed in a baggy suit, but not any kind of suit Mattie had ever seen. This suit was made of two-inch square patches of every color of the rainbow and then some. Mattie couldn't see a single color that repeated anywhere.

"That one is like Dolly Parton threw up on Wall Street," said Trevor.

Mattie snickered. "A suit of many colors?"

"Indeed."

Mattie watched in awe as person after person disembarked from the bus, each outfit more outlandish than the last. Or *as* outlandish, anyway. Really, none of them could be considered *less* outlandish than the next. And all of the hair-dos were just as insane – most of them were enormous, with a few people thrown in who had opted just to shave their heads instead.

Most of the costumes were also gender-neutral, except for some minimalist ones, where the person's gender was . . . very clear. One guy just had a couple of strategically placed lime green sequins.

Finally, the parade ended and the bus drove off.

Mattie and Trevor just sat in stunned silence for several minutes. The hush was broken when Mattie's phone chirped.

She jumped and fumbled for the device. "It's Giovani. Their second bus just pulled up."

"Here comes another one for us, too," said Trevor, nodding toward the rearview mirror.

Mattie leaned over to look at it. "I don't think I'm ready for another one."

Trevor shrugged. "I can ask them to turn around and come back later if you want."

"That'd be great." She grinned. "We'll have to strip you down first. I doubt they'd deign to speak to someone dressed so ordinarily."

"It's so strange, though," said Trevor. "I mean, the agents we've encountered weren't dressed like that."

"The agents have to interact with the outside world," Mattie pointed out. "And they do tend to have kind of a weird fashion sense anyway. Lots of tight clothing, lots of black, and some of them are all about leather or vinyl. Even Giovani's got his bland suit camo situation."

"You're right," said Trevor. "It's like everyone has a theme, and most of them picked 'movie assassin' with a little bit of 'spy' thrown in for good measure."

"I would assume that actual spies probably dress normal, you know, to fit in."

"I wouldn't call Giovani's suits abnormal," Trevor mused. "It only gets weird when you see him every day and he's always wearing the same thing."

"The bus is stopping." Mattie gestured to Trevor to stop talking.

"Oh, sorry, am I distracting you from your gawking?"

"I need some inspiration. My wardrobe is getting a little dull."

Trevor's rich laugh filled the car.

Mattie watched eagerly as the doors opened. This was even more entertaining than *Ancient Aliens*.

An elderly person disembarked, leaning on a tall stick that was carved to look like a dragon, with an actual spout of flame spurting from its mouth into the sky. Mattie grinned and settled in for the show.

An hour later, it was starting to get old. "Oh, look," said Mattie, hand resting on her chin. "Another one that looks like a fish."

"Who would think shiny objects could get so monotonous?" Trevor glanced up from his book. "How many busses is that?"

"Three for this door." Mattie checked her phone. "Two each on the eastern and western entrances. One on the south door."

He sat up straighter. "We're expecting eight busses, right?"

"That's what Giovani said. They're just about all here."

She drummed her fingers on the dashboard and watched as the last of the Auditor court exited the bus, followed by a porter pushing some luggage into the building behind them.

Down the street, a growing group of college students was smoking cigarettes and drinking beer on their balconies, gaping at the outrageous fashion show. Their heads turned as the bus drove off, a couple of them pointing as cars jumped out of its way.

Mattie wondered why the court didn't arrive under cover of night. It didn't feel very clandestine of them to be strutting about in broad daylight in those ensembles.

Maybe they figured they were powerful enough to handle a bunch of random passersby. They were probably right. Then again, they weren't going to be much good in a fight in those outfits.

"This is starting to feel very real," she said. A lump settled in her stomach. Those people she'd just spent the past hour laughing at were people she was going to try to kill at the end of the week.

28.

Tillie watched the stream of absurdly costumed courtiers strut down the hallway, heading for their rooms. The corridor was lined with agents, all of them loyal to Agent Miller's rebellion. Tillie herself was dressed as an agent, wearing soft black leather pants and a tight halter top.

She had felt ridiculous until she'd caught her first glimpse of the court.

As the court flowed by, she found herself looking less at outfits and more at faces. Many of them looked haughty, barely glancing at the agents there to welcome them.

Some looked tired, which was reasonable. They'd been on a bus all day and a bus is a bus, no matter how luxurious. Nicole had told her that the court was coming from Nashville, a five-hour drive.

A couple of people actually smiled at her when she caught their eyes. Tillie made a mental note of those people, hoping she wouldn't come face-to-face with them in battle.

But the ones that chilled her to the bone were the dead-eyed, the ones whose expressionless faces showed no spark of anything at all. It went beyond the exhaustion of travel and spoke of a life empty of any meaning, a lack of any compassion or hope. These were the faces of individuals who had never truly lived.

This was the true evil of an organization that held itself apart. Facing these people in battle wouldn't be war or even extermination – these would be mercy killings.

Finally, the last courtiers entered the building, and Tillie relaxed, expecting that the agents and herself would be free to return to their daily lives.

Nicole, standing beside her, caught her eye and shook her head briefly.

Apparently, there was more. Tillie sighed and stood back at attention. Out of the corner of her eye, she saw movement toward the end of the hallway. Turning her head slightly, she saw that agents were bowing, one after another, like The Wave going through the stands at a basketball game.

Corresponding to the motion, a man was walking slowly past, pausing every so often to examine an agent.

"The Pontiff," whispered Nicole out of the side of her mouth.

Tillie studied the man as he approached.

Physically, he wasn't much to look at. He was probably in his early sixties, balding, his face lined more from frowns than smiles. He was dressed relatively simply, in a long green robe, and carried a strange-looking wooden baton, almost like a wand. It had a very ceremonial look to it, actually, and Tillie amended her original impression – it was more like a scepter.

Then she glanced into his black eyes and felt frozen by the raw, biting bleakness held within.

His eyes narrowed and Tillie hastily bowed. She watched his feet as they walked past her, only missing the slightest of beats at her hesitation.

She forced herself to breathe normally and fervently hoped that she hadn't made him suspicious. Nicole straightened beside her and she followed suit.

Down the hall, the Pontiff turned and entered a stairwell, and the pageantry was finally over.

Time to get back to work.

29.

Somehow, the next couple of days passed. Mattie split her time between honing her mage skills and organizing rotas of mages recruited by Giovani and Ida.

It was a depressingly small number. Ida confided to Mattie that they weren't getting as many on board as she'd expected.

The idea that the Auditors were a myth was widespread, and while no one outright laughed at Ida, they were skeptical that Giovani was who he said he was or that he wasn't just delusional from some kind of trauma.

"Other than my own family, the only place I'm making any headway at all is with the sisters who run my old high school," Ida told her. "Those nuns sure are prepared to take down anyone whose leader claims equal footing with the pope, I suppose."

"There are nuns who are mages?" Mattie's eyebrows shot up.

"Dear, there aren't any nuns who aren't," Ida laughed.

Getting that job at Ida's old high school was sounding better and better.

"Yeah, but are nuns really going to be all that helpful? Aren't they mostly pretty—" Mattie cut herself off before finishing with "old," remembering in the nick of time who she was talking to. "Busy?" she finished, lamely.

Ida's sharp black eyes twinkled. "Oh, they'll make time for us. And don't underestimate us 'busy' ladies. You can never beat the element of surprise, I always say. You get a bunch of 'busy' ladies together and people start to lower their weapons and lower their guards and they forget that we've been in mage battles for years before they were even born. We've still got some life in us yet, I suppose."

Mattie grinned. "I suppose you do."

"You just focus on getting your own skills up to par," said Ida. "This is only your second mage battle, and it's probably going to be one for the history books. Well, in certain circles anyway. They probably won't teach about it in public schools. But mages'll hear about it, I suppose, and we want to make sure we come out smelling like roses."

"I don't care what we smell like," said Mattie, gathering all of her bravado. "As long as the Auditors smell like corpses."

Ida lifted her teacup. "I'll drink to that. You're feeling better about that, then, I suppose."

"I'm working on it." Mattie still felt slightly sick at that thought, but she'd noticed over the past couple of days that the more often she forced herself to think of the court as termites, the easier it got. She drained her mug and stood up. "Shall we spar some more?"

Shaking her head regretfully, Ida set down her own cup and stood as well. "I'd better be moseying on home. I have a couple more family members to wrangle, and they'll be coming by this afternoon." She pointed to Mattie. "You work on your shielding some more, dear, and then get some rest. Tomorrow's the big day."

30.

Tillie woke up to her phone's alarm and her lips curved.

This was the morning. Today was the day.

She threw back the covers and swung her legs out of bed. Once she'd started acting as Nicole's lieutenant, it had made sense to move out of her cell and into the wing of the building that comprised the agents' dormitory.

Her room was not much bigger than the cell, but at least it had some furniture, and the bed, while narrow, was surprisingly comfortable. She'd sent Trevor a picture of the room and he had stitched in a suitcase full of clothing for her.

Tillie opened the top drawer of her dresser to grab her work-out togs. She changed quickly and strode down the hall toward the gymnasium. Nicole and several other real agents were already there, going through their morning routines.

The air was charged with excitement and people all around were pushing themselves, working out their nerves, and getting in that last little bit of practice with tricky martial moves before the battle.

Tillie found a spot to herself off to the side and ran through her stretches, then looked around for someone to spar with. She spotted Agent Shezza nearby, and she looked to be about finished with her own warm-up.

She hadn't really spoken with Agent Shezza much since she'd interrogated the woman in her living room and then gotten herself kidnapped.

Tillie jogged over to her. "Hey. You look like you could use a practice opponent, and I'm guessing you wouldn't mind punching me in the face."

Agent Shezza gave her a wary smile. "I guess I owe you an apology."

"Nonsense." Tillie extended a hand. "It's all in the past. Friends?"

After a slight hesitation, Shezza reached out and shook her hand. "All right. I could use a partner."

"Great! I'm Tillie, by the way." Tillie dropped her hand and shook out her limbs before taking up a defensive stance.

Shezza stepped back and planted her own feet in a completely different pose.

Tillie eyed the woman's posture. Definitely not krav maga. Judo, maybe?

"I know who you are," said Agent Shezza.

"Right," said Tillie. She circled her opponent, looking for a weakness to exploit. "I was just wondering what your name is?"

"Shezza." The other woman feinted with a small punch and then landed a kick to Tillie's shoulder.

Tillie danced back slightly, shaking it off. "You're not getting back to your first name like everyone else around here?" She saw an opening and rushed forward, attempting a kick and a punch, only to find herself falling forward as Agent Shezza dodged and pulled her off-balance.

Staggering, Tillie recovered and eyed her opponent with new respect. The woman might be kind of a dumbass, but she could fight.

"I'm not ready," said Shezza. "I shouldn't have to if I'm not ready."

"Of course," said Tillie. She finally managed to land a kick squarely on Shezza's belly. Shezza's breath whooshed from her body and she stumbled back, recovering quickly and darting forward to grab Tillie's arm and flip her down onto the mat. Tillie scrambled to her feet, breathing heavily. "You've been through a lot. Move at your own pace, by all means."

"Thank you." Shezza circled Tillie, watching her closely. "You're holding your own here. That's impressive."

Tillie grinned. "Cocky."

Shezza didn't smile back. "I'm just good and I know it. You and your sister wouldn't have gotten the best of me if you hadn't caught me off-guard."

"We caught you off-guard? You ambushed us in my building!" Tillie aimed a kick at Shezza's chest, but Shezza caught it and twisted, sending Tillie tumbling ass-over-ankles onto the mat once again.

Shezza danced back, waiting for her to get up. "I wasn't expecting two of you, and I knew your sister wasn't a seer. I still thought you were dead at that point."

"Right." Tillie sat up but didn't stand. She lifted her hands. "I surrender. I think I better save my energy to fight the real enemies tonight, and if I don't stop now, I'll just be stiff, sore, and covered in bruises."

Agent Shezza offered Tillie her hand, and she pulled herself to her feet, smiling.

"Yes." Agent Shezza didn't return the smile. "The true abominations will fall tonight."

Tillie returned to her room, feeling a little bit rebuffed, but glad of the exercise she'd gotten. She grabbed a towel and sauntered down to the communal bathroom shared by all of the women on this floor – about half of the female agents in the building.

The other residential wing of the building, the one that hosted the court when they were in town, for a couple of months every few years, had private bathrooms attached to each room. But the agents, even the ones who lived there full-time, had to share. It was little things like that which had added up to Agent Miller's rebellion.

A tale as old as time…. The people who do none of the work reap all of the rewards, while the ones who slave away at their behest get screwed. Until they rise up.

Tillie found an empty shower stall, hung up her towel, and turned on the tap. She stripped out of her sweat-soaked clothing as it heated up, then stepped into the steamy water, perfectly hot, just short of scalding, and began to scrub, deep in thought, going over the plan for that night in her mind.

The ball would begin with a banquet at seven. That's when the rebels would begin to gather. As the Pontiff and his courtiers were stuffing themselves into a stupor, their agents would be rallying, supplemented by the outside mages recruited by Giovani and Ida.

Once the banquet was done, the children of the court would adjourn to their rooms, and the real party would start.

And then the battle would begin. Hopefully, the court would be taken by surprise and it would be over quickly. After that, the invading army would head upstairs to the nursery wing and shuffle the kids out.

Any of the rebels who had progeny among them would be able to claim them. All of the others would be put in the charge of the good nuns at St. Elizabeth Convent, attached to Ida's old high school.

Tillie turned off the flow of hot water and grabbed her towel, drying off her body and carefully dabbing her face and hair. She wrapped the towel around herself and stepped out of the stall, heading for a spot at the mirror.

She had the room mostly to herself, as she'd discovered that her preferred waking time was in between the early birds and the wave of more sluggish late risers. The former were already finished with morning ablutions and had moved on to breakfast, while the latter were still working up a sweat in the gym.

Grabbing a blow dryer, Tillie began to groom herself for battle.

31.

The evening had arrived, and Mattie rode with Trevor to the convent where the troops planned to convene. Her gut felt like it contained a bundle of writhing snakes. Not only was she going to war, but she was going to be meeting a nun today who might be her boss next school year – if said nun took Ida's recommendation and hired Mattie.

It would be the weirdest – and bloodiest – job interview of all time.

Trevor glanced over at her as he pulled his car into the stone-walled parking lot behind a large brick building. "Matts, it's all going to be okay."

"You definitely can't know that," she retorted.

"That's true," said Trevor. "I can't know it. I can't promise it. I can't even assume it. But I can hope it, right?"

"Yeah," she conceded. "But what does it even mean to be okay? In these circumstances, I mean."

He paused. "Well. What I'm hoping is that all of the mages on our side stay alive. That only a few of the mages on their side get killed before all the rest of them surrender and we can just take them prisoner and then get all of those kids out without incident. And also I hope that this Sister Catherine person really digs the cut of your gib and insists on hiring you on the spot."

"That's a lot, dude."

"It could happen." Trevor turned off the car. "In a world where magic is real, all of that is absolutely one hundred percent possible."

"But is it likely?"

"No less likely than all of us getting killed and the Auditors taking over the world." Trevor leaned back in his seat, making no move to get out of the car. "In fact, if you think about it logically —"

"Does that seem like something I would do?" said Mattie.

"Not really. But all I'm saying is that because we're prepared and they're not, it's far more likely that we will prevail. And since you're amazing, it also seems likely that Sister Catherine will hire you."

"I'm glad we're friends, Trevor." Mattie smiled, her stomach already feeling calmer. "And if either of us doesn't make it out tonight – I just want to make sure you know how much I love you."

Trevor turned so he was sitting sideways against the back of his seat and reached out a hand, gripping her shoulder. "Of course I know that, silly. And you know that I love you too."

Mattie regarded him fondly. "If we have to go to war, at least we can fight beside our true friends."

"Well said. Shall we?" Without waiting for a response, Trevor twisted back around, opening his door and exiting the car in one swift movement.

Mattie followed suit and they joined the grim-faced flow of mages streaming toward the horseshoe-shaped building.

A smiling woman in blue jeans and a navy blue nun's whimple – Mattie had looked up the name of the headscarf thingy earlier that day – waved to them from an open door off to their left and they approached.

"Hello! Welcome! I am Sister Catherine," she said. "And you are . . . ?"

"Trevor Harper and Mattie Holiday," said Trevor.

The woman ran the end of a pen down the edge of the clipboard she held and then inverted the writing utensil to mark off the names. "Well, it's a pleasure to meet you both, but especially you, Mattie! I understand you're interested in teaching English with us next year!"

"Yes. If we don't die," said Mattie.

Sister Catherine laughed. "I'm sure rooting for you." She waved them into the building, pointing across the gymnasium to a cluster of metal folding chairs arranged in front of a stage. About half of the chairs were occupied. "We're gathering yonder. Take a seat and we'll begin shortly."

"Thanks. Nice to meet you," said Mattie. She led the way to a pair of empty seats. "We'll begin what, exactly?" she said to Trevor as he sat down beside her.

He shrugged. "Beats me. Honestly, I always just assumed we'd be meeting up at the Auditor HQ."

"Battle virgins, huh?" said a dry voice to Mattie's right.

She turned to see a busty Latina woman about her own age lounging on one chair with her legs propped up on another. On her lap was some kind of sharpening apparatus and she was currently engaged in lazily drawing a wicked-looking blade across its surface.

"Uh, yeah, I guess," said Mattie.

"We don't convene at the battleground because we want to make sure everyone is ready and because there are always last-minute organizational details to iron out," said the woman. She continued rhythmically honing her knife as she spoke. "We'll get everyone together, break up into teams of three – one speller, one stitcher, one seer in each group to maximize effectiveness. And then we'll get carpools set up, making sure there's enough transport available to take care of any injured at the end of the night – Sister Catherine usually takes those in our van."

A suspicion floated into Mattie's head. "I'm sorry, did you just say 'our' van?"

The other woman paused, examining her blade closely before responding. Then she set the knife down on her table among an impressive assortment of bladed weapons, swung her legs down to the floor, and turned to face Mattie and Trevor with a roguish grin. "Sure did." She extended a hand toward Mattie. "Sister Margaret. At your service."

Mattie grinned back and shook the proferred hand. Sister Margaret's hand was warm and dry, her shake firm. "Pleased to meet you."

"You're a nun?" said Trevor. "Aren't you a little –" He stopped, clearly at a loss for words.

She smirked at him. "Young? Hot? Bloodthirsty?"

"Yes." Trevor nodded vigorously. "Those."

She shrugged. "I know there are fewer people in our generation taking vows, but there are probably more of us than you think. And, yeah, some of us are pretty bloodthirsty. We join up to be warriors for Christ. As far as my looks go, I can't help how God made me. But as long as you don't hit on me, don't try to claim my

vow of celibacy is a 'waste,' and don't try to convince
me that all I really want is a fucking passel of babies,
we'll get along fine."

Trevor smiled. "Oh, believe me, as an equally good-
looking asexual man, I am familiar with the sting of
accusations like that."

"Wonderful." Sister Margaret grabbed another
weapon, this one a short sword, and repositioned the
whetstone on her lap. She began to sharpen it.

"Are you really going to be carrying all of those
tonight?" asked Mattie.

"You better believe it," said Sister Margaret. "These
fuckers think they can go around kidnapping innocent
mages *and* their leader has stolen one of the titles of our
Holy Father? Bitches are gonna get filled with holes,
courtesy of yours truly."

"Can I be on your team?" said Mattie.

"Are you a seer?"

"Speller. And I can do a little bit of stitching."

"Damn straight you can be on my team," said Sister
Margaret. "How about you, Trevor?"

"I'm a stitcher, but I think I'll probably try to get on
Tillie's team," he said. "Thanks anyway."

"Tillie?"

"My best friend," said Trevor. "Mattie's sister. She's
currently infiltrating the Auditor headquarters,
pretending to be an agent."

Sister Margaret whistled. "Bad-ass. Glad to have
you all aboard."

32.

The rest of Tillie's day was spent meeting with Nicole, Aaron, and other leaders about the final logistics of the evening's attack. Most of their co-conspirators were engaged in setting up the ballroom for the banquet and the dance that would follow. Along the way, they'd be installing traps and distractions to give their group that much more of an edge.

Most of the agents were discharged from their station duties mid-afternoon. Some of them would be required to serve dinner as well and would slip out to join the others as soon as the tables were cleared to make room for the ball.

Finally, early in the evening, Nicole dismissed them to get some rest and prepare for the upcoming battle.

Tillie left the meeting room, an uneasy feeling causing her to fidget as she walked. What was making her so nervous? She switched into seer mode, but abruptly switched back as she was bombarded by an onslaught of varying visions.

Too many possibilities to see any one outcome.

She turned a corner, heading toward the stairs that led up to her room, and found herself face-to-face with none other than the Pontiff.

Tillie gasped and stared at his cold face.

The Pontiff frowned and she belatedly and hastily bowed. "I'm sorry, Your . . . Eminence," she said. Was 'Eminence' correct? She tried to remember if anyone had ever told her.

"Rise, child," he intoned.

Child? Screw this condescending prick. If she wasn't already planning to take him down, that would have clinched it.

Tillie pasted a bland smile onto her face and straightened from her bow.

"Now. I have an errand for you, Agent . . . ?"

"Holiday," said Tillie.

An odd look passed across his icy visage. Did he recognize her name? Maybe she should have said something else. How could he have?

"Agent Holiday? I don't think I know that name," he said, thoughtfully. "I was certain I knew all of the names of the agents present here."

"I just arrived yesterday," she said. "Chasing down an abomination from Tulsa."

"Ah. How fascinating. Was your quarry caught?" He leaned toward her, his lips tightening in a small, smug smile.

"Yep," said Tillie, desperately hoping he wasn't going to ask her for any details. "He'll be learning the error of his ways in no time."

The Pontiff clapped his hands softly. "Wonderful! You're doing wonderful work, Agent Holiday. And now, if you could deliver this to Agent Shezza?" He produced an envelope from the sleeve of his golden robe. "I believe she will be upstairs in her room, preparing for her duties serving at my head table this evening. Room 415, if I'm not mistaken."

"Oh. Sure." Tillie gingerly took the missive from the Pontiff's left hand. As she did so, his right hand shot out, grasping her wrist in a viselike grip. His fingers were frigid as they dug into her skin.

Startled, Tillie met his piercing gaze.

"See that it gets to her, no matter what," he ordered.

She nodded quickly, trapped in his stare like a cornered rabbit.

"Excellent." The Pontiff finally released her and without another word, strode around her, his heels clicking on the tile floor of the hallway as he left.

Tillie remained frozen for another long moment, her mind racing. Should she take the missive to Shezza? What was so special about Shezza that she was getting messages from the Pontiff? Maybe she should open it.

She examined the cream-colored envelope. It was a non-standard size, as though it contained a Christmas card or a wedding invitation. Turning it over, Tillie wiggled the flap a little to see if it would come up, but it was well-sealed.

Hearing a sound from behind her, Tillie whirled around, half expecting to see the Pontiff returning. Instead, she saw Nicole headed toward her and she lifted an arm, waving the other woman over.

"The strangest thing just happened to me. I think. I don't know. Is it strange that the Pontiff just gave me a letter to take to another agent?"

Nicole frowned. "It's not unheard of, but it's a little odd. Typically, he would send a page. One of the court children. But if they're all busy or in training, it's not unheard of for an agent to run errands. Who is the letter for?"

"Shezza," said Tillie. "The agent who kidnapped me. What do you know about her? She wouldn't tell me her first name."

"She's not alone in that." Nicole shrugged. "There's a handful of agents who aren't ready to embrace the whole first-name thing. It's been a long time for most of us, going by our last names. It's our identity now. As far as what I know about Shezza, I have to admit it isn't much. She's a field agent, so she hasn't spent a whole lot of time here, and I never really got to know her. I know she's been with us since the beginning, for almost five years. I know that Agent Miller trusted her, which has always been enough for me."

Tillie nodded thoughtfully. "That's compelling. I still feel apprehensive about this message, especially given the timing."

Nicole grabbed Tillie's arm lightly and guided her into a meeting room. "Let's take a look."

Tillie placed the letter on the table, and Nicole extended a glowing hand toward it.

Nothing happened to the envelope, and Nicole frowned. "It's protected against spells. I can't open it."

"Is that unusual?" asked Tillie.

Nicole sighed. "I honestly don't know. I've never gotten a letter from the Pontiff, and even if I had, I probably wouldn't have tried a spell on it."

"Let me try something." Tillie reached out her hand and focused intently on moving her fingers into a stitch, concentrating on getting the letter within the envelope to jump out onto the table.

She reeled backward as her energy hit a brick wall of a shield. "Nope."

"What about a combination of seeing and spelling?" Nicole suggested.

"Yeah," said Tillie. She snapped her fingers as a thought occurred to her. "I can try to project what's written on the letter into the air."

She turned on her seer sight and cleared her mind, trying to find words to speak that would set the spell free. She finally settled on a spell and spoke it aloud.

Elaborate cursive writing began to appear in the space above the letter, and Nicole grabbed a pen and paper from the center of the table, scribbling furiously as she copied it down.

Tillie repeated her spell over and over again until Nicole put down her pen; then she released it and collapsed into a chair, exhausted. "What did it say?"

Nicole picked up the page and read aloud. "'Distinguished Agent Shezza, I am pleased to inform you that you have been selected for advancement within the organization. You will appear before the court this Monday morning at nine o'clock sharp to be given your new duties. In order to give you ample time to prepare, you are hereby excused from serving at the high table at this evening's festivities. Yours, Pontiff Allestro.'"

Tillie leaned back in her chair. "What does all of that mean?"

Nicole's face looked troubled. "Honestly, I'm not really sure."

"Shezza's getting a promotion." Tillie tapped her fingertips on her lips. "And she didn't mention anything about it to you?"

"She might not have been aware it was coming," said Nicole. "It often happens that way. Agents are promoted to bureaucratic roles or even to the court with no warning, just because someone in the court noticed that they'd been doing well."

"Wait, I thought the only way someone could be in the court was if they'd been born to it." Tillie frowned. "Isn't that part of why you all got so angry?"

Nicole shook her head. "No, it does happen. It's rare and it's almost always because the agent either betrayed another agent who was doing something wrong or because their kid made it high up in the court and wanted to bring in their parents."

Tillie sat upright. "Betrayed another agent?"

Nicole's eyes widened. "You don't think . . . ?"

"The timing is very suspicious," Tillie noted.

"Yeah, but—" Nicole paused and then shook her head vehemently. "No. And to be honest, it's not even that I don't think she *would* do it – I don't think she's smart enough to do it."

"Fair enough," said Tillie. "So, you think it's just a coincidence?"

"It won't matter after tonight and it's too late to do anything about it before tonight," said Nicole. "If she has betrayed us, we'll all be dead and won't care. If she hasn't, her promotion isn't going to happen, because the court will be no more." She picked up the letter and handed it to Tillie. "Go ahead and deliver it. Then get some rest. You need to recoup your energy after that tricky bit of morphing. And if we've been betrayed, we'll need the extra edge."

Tillie nodded. She did feel tired. "I think I'll stop by the cantina and have some tea first."

"Good idea," said Nicole. "Meet back in the main meeting room on the first floor at seven o'clock. This changes nothing."

33.

By the time they arrived at the Auditor HQ, Mattie and Sister Margaret were great friends. Sister Margaret was the first nun she'd ever known, and she was definitely not what she'd imagined nuns to be like, if she'd ever paused to imagine it at all.

Mattie had found herself assigned to a team with Sister Margaret as the seer and Sister Catherine as the stitcher.

Sister Catherine, while not quite the kindred spirit Sister Margaret was, had turned out to be a warm, encouraging, and enthusiastic woman who carried only slightly fewer weapons than her younger colleague. She had driven her own van, which would also serve as transport for the wounded after the battle.

Sister Margaret had ridden with Mattie and Trevor.

Mattie got out of the passenger seat of Trevor's Subaru to find Sister Margaret already standing on the sidewalk, buckling her swords and knives into place. She wore a short sword at each hip and a longer sword on her back, and, as Mattie watched, she made several knives and daggers disappear all over her person.

All around them, the mages she'd seen back at St. Elizabeth's gym were assembling again – the Garaveldis with their thick eyebrows and mostly grim faces, corralled by Ida, whose face was as cheery as ever. The nuns, monks, and priests, who acted like this was just any other day. Maybe, for them, it was.

Mattie couldn't help but notice that all of the churchy types were heavily armed, while the Garaveldis and a small scattering of other mages carried no visible weapons.

After just a few minutes, everyone was gathered and ready. Now she understood why they had met up in a more neutral location – she'd have hated to be getting organized out here on the sidewalk.

The last straggler hurried up to the group, and then Giovani entered the door code and they trooped inside, marching three deep through the sliding spaceship door and down the hallway.

Once inside, the first team, consisting of Giovani, Ida, and a woman who looked a lot like them, jogged ahead, scouting to make sure it was all safe for the rest of them.

Mattie's team was toward the middle of the pack. She counted about ten teams ahead of her and estimated about the same behind. As Giovani signaled them forward, the small army marched forward in short bursts, moving cautiously through the building.

It should be deserted, as the court would be sitting down to the banquet right now, on the other side of the huge building. But the seers had rightly insisted upon caution. Mattie knew that if she'd been in charge, she would have just launched the whole party straight to their target and probably gotten everyone killed. That's why spellers weren't in charge.

Finally, after about ten minutes of stop-and-start tactics, as Mattie found herself growing more and more tense, they arrived outside the meeting room where the smaller group of rogue agents had gathered.

Giovani and his team went into the room. The rest of the army stayed in the hall.

Sister Margaret's sharp elbow poked into Mattie's side. "Hey. Fidgety. Take some deep breaths. We need you cool and collected come battle time."

Mattie forced herself to stop fidgeting. "Sorry. I'm just getting antsy."

"You just want to go charging in," said Sister Margaret with a grin. "We'll get there soon enough, I promise."

"Too soon, if you ask me," said Sister Catherine on Mattie's other side. "Don't get me wrong – this battle needs to happen, but I'm never looking forward to bloodshed."

"Nor do I," Mattie murmured.

Sister Margaret slapped Mattie's back, causing her to stagger slightly forward. "That's why you've got me along!"

Giovani stepped out into the hallway and called back toward the ranks of mages. "Trevor Harper. You elected to remain without a team so you could join with Tillie, yes? Is there anyone else out here who doesn't have a team?"

Trevor made his way forward, as Giovani scanned the crowd for anyone else. He must have seen a hand raised toward the back, because he gestured impatiently. "All right. Come up here."

A young man squeezed past Mattie and her teammates. He was looking around, taking in everything he saw with great interest, and he didn't really seem to know anyone else. Mattie frowned, cocking her head as she studied him.

He didn't look like a Garaveldi – he was a little too . . . delicate. Must be with the churchy types. A seminary student, maybe? He reached the front of the group.

"And you are . . . ?" said Giovani.

The young man – kid, really, barely out of his teens – gave Giovani a dazzling smile. Giovani took a small step back.

"Sammy," said the kid, oozing confidence. He held out a hand to shake. "And aren't you a strapping fellow?"

"Right," said Giovani, shaking the guy's hand briefly and then dropping it. "Any chance you're a speller?"

"I can be whatever you want me to be." Sammy winked.

"Oh, a morpher!" Giovani nodded. "Perfect. You can round out this team, then."

Mattie was pretty sure that wasn't what Sammy had meant, and she was pretty sure now that he wasn't a seminary student. But he hadn't said he wasn't a speller, so she had to assume that he could do spells, at least. Maybe he was one of the few unrelated mages Ida had scared up. Whoever he was, looked like he was Tillie and Trevor's problem now.

In fact, he had moved on to regarding Trevor, looking him up and down in a blatantly frank appraisal. "So," he said. "Tall, dark, and striking. What's your deal?"

Unbelievable. This guy was flirting, in the middle of an actual coup against an international cabal of mages. Beside Mattie, Sister Margaret snorted.

"Ace," replied Trevor shortly.

"Fair enough," said Sammy.

That was good. Trevor got very grumpy whenever someone wouldn't take no for an answer. Tillie also got very protective of Trevor, and Mattie noticed that her sister was now standing beside Trevor, giving Sammy the stink-eye.

Mattie turned her attention back to Giovani, who stood in the doorway, addressing both groups, in and out of the meeting room. "Thank you, everyone, for being a part of this historic day," he began.

"Oh, skip the pep talk," interrupted Ida. "We're already peppy, and we're on a time crunch. Let's just get moving!"

There was a murmur of agreement from pretty much every speller in the corridor, including Mattie. Sister Margaret laughed as Giovani lifted his hands in surrender.

"Fair enough," he said. "We all know the plan?"

"Yes!" bellowed the gathered mages.

"All right! Let's do this!" He gestured toward the mages inside the room and then stepped back, falling into formation with his team at the head of the column. Directly behind him, Tillie, Trevor, and Sammy formed their line.

And the rebel agents began to pour out of the meeting room in their own teams, led by Agent Poe and two others.

34.

Tillie watched her co-conspiring agents stream out of the meeting room. It felt right that she was no longer part of that group, instead standing here beside Trevor. She sort of wished Mattie was on her team too but was glad to have another morpher around, even if this Sammy person did keep glancing at Trevor somewhat lasciviously.

There was no harm in that specifically, but he better not try to hit on Trevs again, or she would rain down hellfire. And he better not get distracted mid-battle. This was too important.

The rebel Auditor agents numbered far fewer than the army gathered to back them up, and soon, the last team among them – Agent Shezza, Danielle, and a seer Tillie only vaguely recognized – was marching, and Giovani's team was following.

Tillie gripped Trevor's hand and marched forward toward the battle.

Suddenly, the army stopped. Tillie waited, expecting that they were simply pausing to open the doors and would be charging any moment. A minute ticked by.

"What's going on?" asked Trevor. "I can't see around the corner."

Tillie turned on her seer sight.

"Hey, cool!" said Sammy, on her other side, as her eyes went white. "How'd you do that?"

Frowning, Tillie glanced over at him and froze. Her sight was showing Sammy cowering in a corner of the ballroom, shaking in fear while the battle raged. "What the hell?" she hissed. "You're not a mage!"

She saw herself standing in front of him, warding off the attacks of court mages.

In real-time, Trevor let out a stream of curses.

"Sure I am." A note of uncertainty entered Sammy's heretofore confident voice. "We're all mages, right? Did I get the story wrong?"

Trevor grabbed the kid's arms and pushed him against the wall.

In the future, Tillie saw Trevor fall in battle, without her by his side. Her breath caught.

"This isn't some kind of role play! How did you get in here?" Trevor demanded.

In the present, Tillie pulled Trevor off of Sammy, tugging them both toward a meeting room.

Mattie paused as they passed. "What's going on? Is something wrong?" she called out.

"Yes," said Tillie, through gritted teeth. "No time to explain." As she altered the future, she saw herself and Trevor leaving Sammy in the empty room and going into battle without him, Trevor no longer in grave danger without her to watch his back.

"Stay in here for thirty minutes," she ordered. "Then make your way out of the building and forget you ever saw us."

"But what's going—"

"Just do it!" she snapped.

Tillie and Trevor returned to their spot directly behind Giovani and Ida.

As they made their way through the ranks, she noticed that Mattie and her team had also moved forward and were conferring with Ida.

Tillie tapped Giovani on the shoulder and he turned around. "What's wrong? Where's what's-his-name? Flirty Boy?"

"Sammy is no longer part of this campaign," said Trevor. "We're not sure how he got in. He's not one of us."

Giovani let out an impressive stream of profanity.

Ida raised an eyebrow at him. "Well, what's done is done, I always say. You got him out of the line of fire, I suppose?"

"Yes," said Tillie.

"That's all we can do. Now I don't suppose either of you seers wants to tell me what the hell is holding us up here?"

"Oh, right." Tillie remembered that was why she'd turned on her seer sight to begin with. She focused on the battle, but there were too many factors now that the immediate anomaly had been dealt with. She focused instead on the hallway ahead, metaphysically peering around the corner. "Son of a fuck!"

"What is it?" said Trevor.

"There are guards posted at the door," said Giovani grimly, his own eyes gone white as well. "A lot of guards. It looks like they were expecting trouble."

"Expecting it?" Trevor murmured. "Visions were dampened. Do you think we have a mole?"

"None of us is a dirty fucking rat," averred Sister Margaret. "You can count on that."

Sister Catherine agreed. "Not on my watch, anyway. And no one under Ida Garaveldi's watch would dare either." She nodded deferentially toward Ida. "It has to be one of the rebel Auditors."

Tillie grimaced. Shezza. It had to be Shezza. She started to speak, but a flash of the future presented itself to her – Shezza among flames stitching a grey-clad child out of danger and then returning for another, among a whole crowd of frightened kids.

Something else was going to go wrong later and Shezza was needed. And why would she be saving the court children if she had been the one to betray them? Tillie ran her magically-enhanced eyes over the crowd of rogue agents in front of her but saw nothing that would indicate betrayal.

Still, it made the most sense that it would have been an agent – what would any of the outside mages have to gain? And how would they even have gotten to the court to snitch in the first place?

It could even have been that one of the agents Nicole had sent away had figured it out and blown the whistle before they'd left.

Tillie turned off her seer sight as the chaos of the uncertain futures became overwhelming. She heard a sound from the head of the corridor and turned her attention forward.

Nicole had levitated herself to float over the army and was starting to speak. "If I could have your attention, please."

The perturbed mages in the hallway quieted.

"It appears the tables have been turned. They are expecting us. We have guards to fight here, outside the ballroom, and I have no idea what kind of scene will await us once we fight our way through those. At this point, those of us who are part of the organization are trapped. Retreat is not an option for us. If we try to flee, the court will hunt us down. So we will stay and fight, regardless of the changed odds. The rest of you are free to go or stay as you please."

She paused and the hall filled with a tangible silence as the mages processed her speech.

A slight *whoosh* came from just behind Tillie and she turned to see that Sister Margaret had unsheathed the two swords she'd carried on her hips. "My blades and my life are dedicated to the defense of the innocent." The warrior-nun's voice rang out clearly. She lifted her swords, indicating each as she named them. "St. Joan and St. Quiteria remain thirsty for the blood of your enemies."

"Well-spoken, Sister," said a priest a few rows back. "The Church will fight for this cause, and if we die, we will take our reward in the afterlife."

A few cheers broke out from other nuns, priests, and monks.

Ida stepped forward as well. "Any Garaveldi who wants to leave can do so, but you won't be invited to my house for Christmas this year."

None of the Garaveldi mages cheered, but none of them left either. Ida waited a moment and then turned back to address Nicole. "Looks like we're all still in too."

"And the Holidays as well," said Tillie. She didn't even need to check with Mattie. Not because they were twins and had some sort of weird twin sense of what the other was thinking. She just knew Mattie wasn't one to back down. And of course, Trevor was basically a Holiday too.

Nicole bowed her head. "All of your continued support means everything to us. We charge on my signal." She twisted in place, still floating above the crowd. She lifted her hands.

Tillie tensed, ready to surge forward along with the rest of the army. Then a thought crossed her mind. "Wait!" she called out.

Nicole turned again.

"There are only about fifty guards," said Tillie. "We outnumber them."

"Yeah, but they have the spatial advantage," said Nicole. "We're in a bottleneck and they're in the antechamber."

"But what if we split up?" Tillie countered. "There are three hallways that lead into that antechamber. Agents stay where they are and attack from this hall, since you're already up front there. The rest of us split up and the teams with the strongest stitchers go to the western entrance. The others run around to the east side. Once everyone is in position, we attack from three sides."

"I love it," said Nicole. "Let's go." She turned and floated herself back around the corner, presumably to take command of her agents once more.

Giovani began splitting up the Garaveldis into those who could stitch their teams out and those who couldn't, while Sister Catherine did the same with Team Catholicism.

Tillie turned to Trevor, who lifted his hands in a gesture of warding. "Don't look at me. I have never stitched three people before, and I don't think this is the time to be experimenting."

"Let's head to the eastern hall, then." Tillie grabbed his hand again and began tugging him in that direction.

35.

Mattie waited for Sister Catherine to tell her which direction their team would be going in.

Finally, the head nun finished her count and conferred with Giovani. Then she jerked her head toward all of her charges, Mattie included. "Come on, the Garaveldis have the stitching covered. Regardless of your talents, we're heading toward the east hall."

"I know how to get there," Mattie volunteered. The east hall was where she and Trevor had gotten lost the first time they'd been in the building. She led the way around a couple of corners and then finally came to the closed door that led to another short hallway that emptied out into the antechamber outside the ballroom.

She reached for the door, but Sister Margaret grabbed her hand. "Don't be a complete dumbass. I'll check it out."

Sister Margaret's eyes turned white as she peered into the hallway. "All clear. The fuckers must be stationed just at the ballroom itself."

Mattie followed the nun into the corridor, the rest of their group streaming after her. Tillie and Trevor had gotten a head start and were already there waiting for them.

Sister Margaret, her seer eyes still going, held up a hand. "Shit. The bastards have more in reserve, and the motherfuckers are going to come streaming out of the ballroom as soon as we attack."

"What if we don't attack en masse?" suggested a grizzled older priest who walked with a limp. "What does it look like if we keep mostly out of sight and send in one speller at a time to knock a few out and then retreat? Just chip away at them."

Sister Margaret's eyes sort of flickered as she reevaluated. "Good idea, Father Sean. That could work."

Mattie pulled her phone out of her pocket. "I'll check in with Giovani about this new plan." She shot off a text and the tension mounted as the group waited for the response.

She jumped as the phone chirped. "It's a go. They'll send someone at the same time. And he'll notify the agents to do the same."

The phone chirped again and she read the new text. "Okay, spellers, line up. We'll go one at a time. Duck in, hit 'em with your best spell, then duck out, and the next speller goes right after." The phone chirped again. "Seers, keep watching and let us know if we should change tactics."

"And stitchers?" asked Trevor.

Mattie typed in a query. It was answered quickly. "Stand by and save your energy for healing."

"Got it."

"I'll go first," said Mattie. She handed her phone to Trevor. "You can hold onto this since you'll just be standing by. Keep in touch with the boss."

Mattie waited until the other spellers were lined up behind her. Then she waited for Trevor to let her know that it was time. She waited a good thirty seconds and then turned toward him. "Nothing from Giovani?"

"I'll check in." He typed something and the response came in. "Oh, he was waiting for you. Go ahead!"

Mattie threw open the door and shoved her glowing hands out in front of her, a huge gust of wind emanating from them. That should confuse them and allow the next guy to deliver a more effective killing blow.

She was startled to see that the guards were all garbed in a ridiculous uniform of bright orange panels of some kind of metal interlocking across their chest and groin like a robot's idea of a hula girl outfit. Mattie knew that the court favored bizarre outfits, but that just seemed incredibly impractical.

Refusing to be distracted for long, she peeled off from the line, hurrying to the back.

They moved quickly, each speller tossing one spell toward the guards and then rushing out of the way of the next one. Mattie found herself back at the front of the line just a couple minutes later, and she readied a lightning spell.

Father Sean lumbered out of the way and she stepped forward. Her eyes darted across the chaotic room until she saw an upright figure. She jabbed the lightning at him and he fell.

She hurried back to the end of the line behind Father Sean and readied her next spell.

"Watch out!" shouted Tillie.

At the same time, Sister Margaret yelled, "Incoming!"

Mattie's head snapped around, just in time to see three stitchers in the same crazy colorful armor blink in. Her arm shot out and she threw the lightning she had ready at the closest one. As spellers reacted, the enemy stitchers all fell.

"Another wave!" warned Tillie.

Mattie saw Sister Margaret pull a knife from her sleeve and toss it to Trevor, just before the new stitchers blinked in.

He caught it and stabbed one of the newcomers in the man's unprotected belly. The guard fell immediately, blood gushing. What a ridiculous armor design – why would they have such a weird gap? And when had Trevor learned how to use a dagger?

"Spellers!" Mattie ordered. "Stay in line – this is obviously working or they wouldn't be trying to disrupt it! Stitchers and seers, watch our backs!"

"Great plan, Mattie!" said Sister Catherine. She had drawn one of her own blades and was slashing the throat of an Auditor guard. "Keep up the good work." The nun whirled around and stabbed another adversary in the gut.

Mattie readied another lightning strike and dashed through the door, taking down another two guards outside the door. As she rushed back into the hall, she saw that stitchers were still coming in and the battle was starting to rage as the enemy stitchers outnumbered their own.

She returned to her spot in the speller queue. While she waited for her turn to come again, Mattie began to rotate in place, throwing lethal spells toward the

Auditor stitchers wherever she saw an opening. At least they were easy to spot – there would be no chance of friendly fire, as long as the enemy was dressed in brightly colored and highly impractical armor bikinis.

Before she knew it, it was time for another strike at the door. She leaped through the doorway and stopped short. The way was clear. All of the Auditor guards were down.

Mattie tossed a salute toward the speller who was coming out of the western hallway. "We've got some attackers in here," she called out to him. "Are you guys able to help?"

"Yeah, I think so," the young Garaveldi mage called back. He stuck his head back through the doorway, presumably to address Giovani.

Without missing a beat, Mattie strode back into the corridor. "The door is clear! Let's clear out these bastards and then storm the place!"

Mattie saw Sister Margaret dodging the sword of an Auditor and she flung a lightning bolt toward him. The man fell and Sister Margaret whirled around, punching another attacker in the throat.

Raising shields, Mattie accounted for three more before their back-up swarmed through the door, making short work of the attackers.

"Any injuries?" asked Giovani. "Is everyone accounted for?"

Without waiting for a response, he began counting Garaveldis.

Beside Mattie, Sister Catherine was counting clergy. A leather-clad woman nearby was doing the same with the rogue Auditors.

Mattie shrugged and began counting her own group. It was small, but Tillie and Trevor were both accounted for and neither seemed injured, although they were leaning against each other.

She made her way over to them. "Everyone okay here?"

Tillie smiled. "You're becoming quite the general, Mattie."

"A real leader," Trevor agreed. He was cleaning the knife he'd been using with a piece of cloth. "It would have been chaos in here if you hadn't marshaled the spellers to keep going."

"Yeah, well, it just made sense." Mattie turned and surveyed the rest of their invading army. No new major injuries. And she didn't notice any gaps – it would seem that they'd made it through this unexpected setback without any casualties.

Giovani raised his voice and Mattie turned her attention toward him. "Okay, mages! We're back on track to attack the ballroom! Remember that since they seem to have been expecting us, we may not be able to take them by surprise. This is going to be more challenging than we originally anticipated."

As he spoke, Mattie saw Sister Catherine stitching out with a couple of injured mages. She glanced around to see if there were any actual corpses and was relieved to see only the Auditor guards and no friendly fallen mages.

Giovani continued. "Our army is small and for all we know, they were able to bring in reinforcements. They may have a larger force than we counted on."

Ida nudged him aside. "You're terrible at pep talks, young man." She faced the group and beamed at them.

Mattie felt herself grinning back.

"Listen up, troops," Ida began, arms swinging wide. "We may be outnumbered. We may have lost our element of surprise. But we are better than them! We are seasoned warriors, most of us. And there will be some warriors in there, I suppose, but they are not warriors like we are. Those are court Auditors. They are soft and weak and have hidden behind their agents for too long.

"There will be a lot of people in there. Very strangely-dressed people. These people have been hiding and sneaking around. They have been holding themselves separate from our world, and yet they have dared to steal innocent mages away from our world, simply because they don't like their way of doing things. How dare they? These are kidnappers! Brainwashers! Cultists!"

Ida's smile grew feral, her lips twisting into an angry rictus, her eyes wide. She raised both fists into the air. "We are here to take them down!"

And with that, she turned on her heel and led them down the hall toward the ballroom.

"Yeah!" Mattie roared. All around her, the hallway erupted in cheers as the group flowed after the old woman, ranked once again in their teams of three.

Mattie felt like she could take on the world. She marched toward the ballroom with fire in her heart and spells at the ready.

36.

Tillie charged into the ballroom. Since she and
Trevor didn't have a speller, they had joined forces
with Mattie, and the nuns on Mattie's team had filled in
other teams that had lost members to injury during the
anteroom skirmish. They had been toward the back of
the army, so the great room was already in chaos by the
time she arrived, spells and weapons flying. A wall of
leather-clad Auditor agents five or six ranks deep had
formed between the attackers and the courtiers.

She didn't recognize any of them. Giovani must
have been right about the court calling in the cavalry.

Another defensive line of courtier spellers was
positioned just behind the agents, holding shields
between the attackers and the front lines. Behind them
was the rest of the court, including a small group of
even more extravagantly dressed mages on a dais. The
Pontiff and his inner circle, presumably.

The big wigs were surrounded by another group of
guards in their bright orange, bizarrely designed
armor, waiting and ready for the fight to reach them.

All of her compatriots were attacking the outer
circle of agents, but Tillie had an idea. She switched
into seer sight to run through the scenario, and her lips
curved into a satisfied smile. Grabbing Trevor's hand,

Tillie pulled him off to the side and then darted back into the midst of the battle, dodging blows and spells, to drag Mattie out too.

"What the hell?" Mattie demanded.

"Just listen to me," Tillie urged. "Look up there." She nodded toward the dais. "We want to cut off the viper's head? That's the real head. This is all just distraction."

"Yeah, but how—"

"Trevor, could you stitch the three of us in there?" Tillie interrupted.

"I've never stitched three people before," he said doubtfully. "I honestly don't think—"

"We'll lend you our strength," said Mattie.

He hesitated still.

"I think you can do this, with our help. It's only a short distance and you can see the destination," urged Tillie. "You've got the talent and we'll give you strength."

Finally, he nodded. "I guess we'll never know unless we try."

Tillie took his left arm as Mattie grasped the other. She pushed mage power toward Trevor and felt him accept it.

And then, suddenly, she was behind the line of spellers, looking at the back of a mage who was dressed in a yellow caftan with shapes cut out of it through which some kind of scaly green armor peeked out. Tillie staggered as she adjusted to her new position, letting go of Trevor's hand and reaching out to steady herself on the nearest object – Caftan Guy's shoulder.

She realized what she had done and swiftly tugged on the man's arm, pulling him off-balance and whirling to land a kick on his neck. He fell without a sound and Tillie moved on to the next foe as her seer sight warned her of an incoming spell.

Ducking, Tillie evaded the lightning bolt and flung a fireball of her own toward the woman who had attacked her. It deflected harmlessly off a shield and fizzled out on the black marble floor.

"Abomination," the woman hissed.

"Your outfit is an abomination," said Tillie, throwing another fireball, this time aiming toward the hem of the speller's voluminous skirt. Apparently, her shields didn't extend that far, because the whole purple and pink monstrosity went up in flames immediately.

The mage shrieked and then suddenly disappeared.

What the —? Had she just stitched out of there? Had she seriously just called Tillie an abomination for seeing and spelling at the same time when she herself was spelling and stitching? What a fucking hypocrite!

Filled with rage, Tillie moved on to the next courtier and then the next, kicking, punching, and throwing fireballs with reckless abandon. She mowed her way through enemy after enemy, barely noting the battle raging around her in her state of berserk.

A part of her mind dimly wondered why she hadn't reached the Pontiff yet – surely she had defeated the small group that had been huddling in front of his dais by now. Tillie lifted her head as she dispatched another courtier and realized that she had actually been moving further away from the Pontiff, cutting her way through the line of spellers that had been in the middle of the room.

She whirled and began making her way back toward the dais, catching a glimpse of that familiar chilling face in the middle of a cluster of heavily-armed mages who were still simply waiting, ready to defend the man. They were dressed in the same strange uniform as the mages who had been waiting in the hall outside.

Right in front of the dais, Mattie and Trevor had been joined by Sisters Catherine and Margaret and that limping priest. The five of them were holding their own against the garish courtiers. The floor around them was littered with bright-clad bodies.

Tillie fought her way to their side. How had she gotten so off-track?

"Welcome back," said Trevor through gritted teeth as he stitched aside a fireball thrown at him by a smooth-scalped courtier. He had picked up a sword at some point and slashed it toward the speller, cutting him down with a spurt of blood.

"Die, you fucking shitsucker," screamed the younger nun, her eyes white as she slashed her double swords toward a courtier, slitting his throat.

She must have been hanging out with Mattie.

Tillie turned her attention to a new foe, dodging a spell and attacking with fists and feet. For each Auditor they slew, another took their place.

And these courtiers seemed determined to drive them back toward the door, away from their precious Pontiff. Tillie found herself inadvertently retreating with each Auditor she fought, and she redoubled her efforts to move forward toward the dais.

The good news was that as she fought she noticed more and more of her compatriots fighting around her, which had to mean that the rest of the army was making their way through the forward lines.

Tillie found herself fighting alongside Ida Garaveldi, who moved slowly but fought fiercely, cutting her way through the Auditors with blades of energy that emanated from her glowing hands.

Abruptly, Tillie's mage sight warned her to catch the older woman, and she spun around, arms ready, searching for a wound. She sighed in relief to see that Ida was unharmed. She must have just lost her balance and stumbled. Heaven knew the floor was slippery enough, coated in blood and guts as it was at this point.

Marble was no floor for a battlefield.

"Christopher," Ida whispered as Tillie steadied her.

"What?" Tillie bent her head to hear better.

Ida pointed a shaky finger toward an ancient man standing against the wall of the ballroom. He was half-hidden behind a curtain, throwing spells into the fracas and then ducking back undercover. He must have been a hundred years old if he was a day.

Tillie's arm was still wrapped around Ida's waist, and she felt the old speller regain her balance and her steel. She let go and followed Ida toward the curtain.

Ida threw the drape aside. "Christopher!" Her clear, strong voice rang out.

The man studied her for a moment and then his face twisted into a strange sneer, as though he wanted to smile but couldn't remember how. "Ida Garaveldi. As I live and breathe. You look terrible."

"And you do live and breathe, don't you?" said Ida. "Christopher. I searched for you. I thought you were dead, long ago. I certainly would have thought you'd be dead by now, I suppose, regardless."

"I told you not to look for me, if I recall," said Christopher. "I left you a note."

The pieces of the puzzle clicked into place in Tillie's mind. Trevor had told her Ida's sad story – about her aunt Ines and Ines' fiancé Christopher, who had disappeared within a couple months of each other back when Ida was young.

"As you can see," he continued, "I was fine."

"Fine?" Ida took a step backward. "You're an Auditor. And Ines is as well, I suppose."

"Ines is dead. Fifteen years ago now. She was a fine agent. A fine Auditor. And our son. Well. Our son has done very well for himself."

"Your son?" Ida moved forward again. "Your son would be a courtier, then."

Christopher finally managed to smile. "Our son is *the* courtier." He raised a slightly shaky finger.

Tillie turned her head to see where he was pointing. Oh, no. She closed her eyes, but her seer sight was on. She could still see everything, imprinted upon her eyelids.

The Pontiff was Ida's cousin. This couldn't be good.

37.

Mattie gritted her teeth. These bastards kept forcing her back away from the dais. That was where the Pontiff was, and he was the one they absolutely needed to take out. She threw another lightning bolt at the mage in front of her, but they dodged and ducked, no matter what she did, their white eyes sensing everything before she even knew what she was going to do. It was beyond frustrating.

Finally, Trevor and Sister Catherine noticed her and ganged up on the seer with her. Trevor dispatched the courtier and the three of them moved determinedly back toward the Pontiff and his circle of guards.

And then Sister Margaret was abruptly in front of them, her arms lifted to stop them, hands open, for once empty of any weapons. Mattie halted – if the seer knew something she didn't, she wasn't going to argue.

"What do you see?" asked Sister Catherine.

Sister Margaret pointed toward the side of the room and Mattie turned her head to see her sister and Ida Garaveldi talking to … a curtain? She frowned and stepped toward them. There was an old man behind the curtain. A courtier, although slightly more conservatively dressed. His suit was bright pink, but it was still a pretty normal suit, otherwise.

He was definitely the oldest person in the room, older even than Ida.

Mattie turned back to Sister Margaret. "What's going on?"

Sister Margaret just shook her head, so Mattie jogged toward Tillie.

"This changes nothing," said Ida. "You're not the Christopher I knew."

Whoa. This was Christopher?

"I am who I am," said the old man.

"But you are not who you were. The man I knew died decades ago, I suppose." Ida raised her glowing hands. "And the man you are now dies today."

She made a quick move and a blade of energy flowed from her hand, cutting off the old man's head.

Mattie took an involuntary step back and almost fell, tripping over a corpse's arm. She glanced down at the still face and recognized the Garaveldi eyebrows. She didn't know which Garaveldi it was. But it reminded her that she was in the middle of a battle, and not a moment too soon, as a bolt of lightning hit her shields. She reinforced them and threw a fireball back at the speller, following it up with a jab of lightning as his shields faltered, taking him down.

Mattie looked around for her next opponent, but she saw only Ida, striding through the room, her face set in a determined grimace, a swathe of carnage following and preceding her as she wielded her blade of energy without mercy.

"This ends now," Ida called toward the dais. "I understand this bastard of a Pontiff is my cousin."

Oh, shit. Was Ida switching sides? Mattie remembered how Ida had reacted when she'd learned of Giovani's son. She was very protective of her family. Then again, she had just decapitated Christopher.

"I want to make one thing clear," Ida continued, sternly. "This changes nothing."

Auditors were lining up in front of the dais, watching her warily, but making no move against her. Invaders fell back behind Ida. Mattie joined Tillie and Trevor in the crowd backing Ida.

"As far as I'm concerned, Ines and Christopher were killed the day your organization kidnapped them. So any progeny they supposedly had after that is actually the son of someone else entirely, and no relation to me. Family is as family does, I always say, and you ordered the kidnapping and brainwashing of a Garaveldi. You're no family of mine."

A shield wall so thick it looked almost solid was forming between Ida and the Auditor guards as they prepared for their last stand.

Ida stopped in front of the wall and slashed at it with her energy blades, which now emanated from both hands.

Tillie reached out a hand and clasped Ida's shoulder. Trevor linked his arm into Tillie's and Mattie promptly followed suit, channeling as much energy as she could muster into Tillie, toward Ida. All around, Garaveldis, nuns, priests, monks, and rogue Auditors followed suit.

Ida punched a hole in the wall of shields and with one wild slash, took down the entire line of Auditors who stood in front of the dais.

As one, the attacking army stepped forward, still holding onto each other, channeling all of their mage power into Ida.

She slashed again and the steely-eyed semi-circle of guards fell without landing a single blow.

The Pontiff stood alone, a proud-faced man of middle age, his cold eyes glittering with malice and defiance. He wore a dressed-up version of his usual roman-emporer-style robes, these ones purple with gold accents.

He met Ida's eyes. "I suppose you think you've won."

"I suppose I think we have."

The Pontiff smiled and his hands glowed briefly. "Finish it, then."

Ida lifted her hands and slashed at him.

His throat slit and he crumpled to the ground.

38.

Automatically, Tillie turned toward Trevor. He was turning to her at the same time, and she caught him up in a hug. His arms encircled her, comforting and familiar, squeezing her tightly. She breathed in his scent, books and spices, as usual, but underneath it was the odor of blood.

Tillie stepped back convulsively.

"What's wrong?" he asked, a worried frown creasing his face.

She shook her head. "I'm sorry – it's not you. I just – you know what? We're on a battlefield. Maybe it's not the time for hugging."

"The battle's over," said Mattie, behind her.

"Is it?" she asked, running a hand over her red hair. She shuddered as the stickiness of the blood tangled her fingers in the curls. "Come on. Everyone else is cleaning up. Let's help."

She gestured to her left, where Sister Catherine was healing someone, aided by Sister Margaret and Father Sean. Somewhere along the way, she'd learned the names of a bunch of Catholic clergy. She wondered idly what they would say if they knew she was a sex worker.

Oh, well. It was unlikely to come up and none of their business anyway. Right now, she and Mattie should be helping Trevor tend to the wounded and dispose of the dead.

Tillie noticed Giovani off to the side rounding up the few courtiers who had survived and were now surrendering. He was sitting them down in a corner and then putting them under a freezing spell. She shuddered. Hopefully, he was making sure that they were in comfortable positions first. Sure, they were the enemy, but that was no excuse for torture, especially after they'd already won.

Distantly, Tillie heard a rumble of thunder. It must be storming outside. It was weird to think of weather happening outdoors when they were here in this windowless stone crypt of a ballroom.

Ida's son Tom was stitching the captives out of the room, one by one. She wondered where they were being taken. Their own wounded were being sent to Sister Catherine's van, she knew, but what about the prisoners? And the corpses?

She decided that was someone else's problem.

An injured courtier touched her leg, and she crouched beside the woman.

"Please," the courtier whispered. "Kill me quickly."

"Trevor," Tillie called. "Over here. I have a live one."

Trevor finished stitching away the corpse of a middle-aged nun. Tillie wondered where he was sending them. Hopefully not her ritual room again.

He stood beside her and moved his fingers in a complex gesture. The cut on the woman's head stitched closed and the bleeding stopped. She gasped.

"Why?" she asked. "Why would you heal me?"

"Because," said Tillie, standing and brushing her hands on her thighs. "We're not actually abominations."

She gestured to one of the Garaveldis who was assisting Giovani. The mage hurried over and helped the newly healed courtier stand, walking her over to the other surrendered Auditors.

They continued, working in groups of three, healing the injured on both sides and stitching out the dead on their own side, of which there were far too many, and yet fewer than she might have expected, considering they had walked into an ambush.

Just as she stood up from the last wounded soldier, Tillie heard another, much louder rumble. It almost sounded like it was out in the hallway, but how could there be thunder inside the building? Her head snapped around and she activated her seer sight.

She gasped as she saw the room in flames. All around her, other seers were expressing their own shock. The 'thunder' must have been bombs going off in remote parts of the building.

Ordinarily, at least one seer would have been warned by a vision, but their own dampening spells had worked against them.

"We gotta get out of here!" she shouted, grabbing Mattie and Trevor by the hand and pulling them toward the door.

"What about the children?" asked Mattie.

"She's right," said Sister Catherine beside them. "The last part of our plan – we have to get the kids out, especially if the building is on fire!"

"Let's do it quickly!" said Giovani. "We're done here anyway."

He strode to the door, the rest of them following closely behind.

Outside, in the hallway, the air was hot and hazy. "The fire has already started," said Mattie. "We need to hurry."

"That's what the Pontiff did," said Trevor. "Right before Ida – you know. His hands glowed. He set a fucking fire. We're lucky it's taken this long to spread. I wonder how – "

"Doesn't matter how," said Giovani shortly. He ran for the stairs and they all ran after him.

The children's wing was on the second story, opposite the adult residential area. Their feet pounded on the tiled floor as they rushed toward their rooms.

Before they got there, they saw a crowd of about a hundred children, led by a handful of teens, crowding the hallways, heading toward the stairwell.

Tillie hoped the others were not too far behind. She pushed her seer sight around the corner and was relieved to see another sea of grey-clad kids heading their way.

The older kids stopped short when they saw the bloody, sweaty invaders.

"Who are you?" demanded a pale-faced red-haired boy, who looked about seventeen.

The children were all dressed in uniform charcoal grey pajamas edged in red piping.

"We're here to get you out of the building," said Giovani, neatly evading the question.

"We're already leaving," the boy retorted.

"Then let's go together." Giovani turned around without waiting for a reply and gestured to his troops to go back the way they'd come.

They turned and began to march back down the hall.

Tillie was now at the back of the group, just in front of the children and Giovani. As they passed an adjoining hallway, a door opened and a familiar head peaked out.

"Sammy?" Tillie stopped walking and grabbed him by the arm, hauling him into their pack. "What the hell are you still doing in here?"

"What the hell happened to you?" he countered.

"In case you hadn't figured it out yet, this is a real situation and we just finished an actual battle," she snapped at him, dragging him along. "You need to come with us. This place is burning to the ground."

"Yeah, I noticed that," he said. He shook his arm free, keeping pace with her. "Do you want to explain exactly what you mean by 'a real situation' and follow that up with what 'an actual battle' entails?"

"You know, I really don't think I do." Tillie rolled her eyes.

At the bottom of the stairs, Giovani pushed his way through to the front of the crowd, leading them to the nearest exit. His eyes went white as he turned his seer sight on.

Tillie did the same and immediately began cursing. The place was surrounded by police, fire trucks, and ambulances. How the hell were they going to get out without being arrested? Without the children being taken into custody by well-meaning social workers who would have no idea how to deal with mages? Or even with children who had grown up in a society completely separate from the outside world?

All around her, seers were swearing up a storm.

"What's going on now?" asked Sammy.

Tillie turned off her seer sight and grabbed his arm again. "Where do you live? Nearby?"

"Yeah, just the next building over. Why?"

She dragged him toward the door. "Giovani!" she called. "This kid lives next door."

Giovani raised an eyebrow. "And?"

Tillie addressed Sammy again. "Do you have any pictures of your place on your phone?"

"Yeah."

She raised her voice. "How many stitchers here can get into a place they've only seen a picture of?"

About fifteen hands raised.

Tillie recognized Agent Shezza among them and narrowed her eyes. Then she remembered what she'd seen of the woman stitching children out of a fire. This must be that scenario. She just needed to set it in motion. "Show them your pictures."

A slow smile spread across Giovani's face. "Son of a bitch. We just might make it." He called out over the crowd. "All stitchers or anyone who can stitch, move to the front here. Including any of the kids over the age of twelve."

Once they'd all gathered, he continued. "Okay, those who can stitch from the photo, take the ones who can't. Then you all come back and start stitching the rest. Spellers and seers, if you can't stitch, you can still help. Lend your strength to the stitchers – we're all fucking exhausted. This is our fourth or fifth wind here, and it's gotta happen fast."

As though to punctuate his point, a tile fell out of the ceiling down the hall, narrowly missing the back of the gathered throng of children. The horde surged forward, shrill voices screaming in startlement.

"Let's move!" Giovani ordered.

The crowd of stitchers who had been examining the photo grabbed another stitcher or two apiece and disappeared.

"What the fuck?" yelped Sammy.

"Magic," said Tillie. "Get used to it. We're all heading to your place."

"It's a studio apartment," he protested. "You're not all going to fit in there."

"How many apartments in the building?" asked Mattie.

Tillie raised an eyebrow.

Sammy shrugged. "I don't know. Twenty?"

"Spellers and seers," said Mattie, lifting her voice. "When we get to the safe house, start knocking on doors to other apartments. Anything that's unoccupied, we break in and use as kid storage."

"You can't just—"

Tillie tapped Sammy on the shoulder and his head snapped toward her. "Yes, we can," she said. "And we will. Because otherwise these kids are doomed."

"But—"

"Shut up, okay?"

He sighed. "Okay."

Trevor stitched back into the hall and grabbed Tillie and Mattie.

Tillie swapped her hand for Sammy's. "Better take him first, before he has a heart attack. I'll go next round."

"Sure." Trevor's voice was weary, and Tillie rested her hand briefly on his shoulder, sending him part of her own small reserve of energy. He gave her a tiny, grateful smile.

She dropped her hand and the three of them disappeared.

39.

Mattie found herself in a tiny kitchenette full of people. She dropped Trevor's hand. "Why do we always end up trapped in burning buildings anyway?" she muttered.

"Look on the bright side," he replied. "We always escape from the burning buildings."

"Yeah, so far," she acknowledged. She lifted her voice. "Okay, who's on breaking-and-entering duty with me?"

A ragged chorus of cheers went up.

Mattie turned to Sammy. "Front door?"

He pointed mutely.

"Any tips on the security of the place?"

Sammy shrugged. "Honestly, it's mostly students. Probably half of them don't lock their doors. Try to walk in before you try kicking down doors."

"We don't kick down fucking doors," said Sister Margaret. "We have fucking magic."

Sammy's eyes widened as he took in the spectacle of Sister Margaret, covered in blood, with her arsenal of bladed weapons.

She grinned at him. "What?"

"Nothing," he muttered, lowering his gaze.

More mages were stitching in, including the first round of children. She noticed Giovani stitching in with a boy about eight years old and giving him a brief hug before stitching back out. The boy had those trademark heavy eyebrows.

"Come on," said Mattie. "We gotta find some more room before this place bursts at the seams."

She led the way out into a dark, grungy hallway. "Let's split up. Everyone pick a door and knock. If someone answers, pretend you're a Jehovah's Witness, and when they slam it shut, move on to the next one. If no one answers, get in, make sure it's really unoccupied, and then leave the door open." Mattie poked her head back into the original apartment. "Hey, we're gonna leave unoccupied apartments open, so just bring people in."

"Why can't you just take people outside?" wailed Sammy. "My neighbors are going to kill me."

"Oh, relax," Sister Catherine scoffed at him. "No one will know you had anything to do with it. And we have to wait until the cops are gone and then trickle out slowly so we don't raise suspicion."

"Jesus, what kind of nuns are you?"

"We are what we are," she said and stitched back to the Auditors' building.

Mattie turned back to the hallway, where mages were knocking on doors up and down. She made her way past them to the next door and knocked briskly.

A perky black girl in tight jeans and a red tank top answered promptly. "Hi!" she said. Then she seemed to realize Mattie wasn't who she was expecting and possibly also noticed that Mattie was disheveled and spattered in blood. "Um, hi," she said again, her smile fading.

"Have you accepted Jesus Christ as your personal savior?" Mattie asked.

"Um, yeah. Definitely already done that. Thanks for asking," said the girl, rolling her eyes. She closed the door with a thud.

Mattie grinned. Effective. She moved on to the next one.

40.

Tillie guided the last of the children to sit on the couch in an apartment down the hall from Sammy's. She looked around for a spot to rest her own weary body. The couch, all of the chairs, and the bed were crowded with kids.

She sank down onto the floor beside the sofa, leaning against the legs of the little girl she had just brought in.

The girl tapped her on the shoulder, and she glanced up. "Yes?"

"Thank you for taking us out of the fire."

Tillie managed a brief smile. "You're welcome." She closed her eyes and leaned her head back.

She felt another light tap on her shoulder. She didn't bother opening her eyes this time, nor did she lift or turn her head. "What is it, sweetie?"

Trevor's amused baritone responded. "Sweetie?"

Tillie's eyes snapped open. "I thought you were a little girl."

"Yeah, I get that a lot."

She closed her eyes again. "You've been working at least as hard as I have. What gives you the right to be so chipper?"

"We're getting ready to leave."

"Oh, thank goodness." Tillie suddenly found the energy to sit up straight. "So, what's the plan?"

Giovani appeared in the doorway. "This apartment is to be evacuated first. Sammy tells us that the girl who lives here is exceptionally cranky and we don't want her to come home and freak out. We'll be stitching the kids out again, putting them on the court busses. We'll take them down to the lobby first to make it easier on the stitchers."

"Where are they going on the busses?" asked one of the rebel Auditor agents.

"They'll go to Saint Elizabeth Convent with Sister Catherine. The nuns there will oversee their education and facilitate their transition into the real world. They'll also be fabricating backgrounds and identities for them so that in time they should be able to lead relatively normal lives. Any of you who have children among them, let Sister Catherine know, and we'll see what we can do about getting you set up as a family unit."

"What about the organization?" ventured a teenage boy. "We belong to the court."

"The court has been overthrown and the Auditor organization disbanded," said Giovani, briskly.

The older children looked stunned. The younger ones looked sleepy.

Tillie hoped the nuns would be able to help the kids understand why and how their entire world had been turned upside down overnight. In the meantime, she was happy to get them onto a bus and out of her own life.

She jumped to her feet and took the hand of the girl she had just placed on the couch. "Come on, sweetie, let's go. Some nice ladies are going to give you a new home."

"Okay," she said. Tillie gave her a gentle push and the girl walked toward the door.

At least they were used to moving around. That might make this easier, at least for the littler ones. Teenagers were already inclined to be difficult. Tillie braced herself and then addressed the older boy who sat on the other end of the couch. "You too. Let's go."

The boy opened his mouth, scowling, but before he could speak, Trevor interrupted. "You don't have to like it. But this is how it is."

"I don't like it," said the boy.

"This is how it is," Trevor repeated.

The boy thought about it for a moment and then nodded. "Fair enough." He stood and followed the line of children who were already being led away by Giovani and the other mages.

Tillie grinned at Trevor. "You'd make a wonderful father."

"I know, right? Maybe I'll adopt one of these."

She nodded toward the teenager. "You seem to have that one cowed."

"Oh, is 'cowed' the goal?" Trevor cocked his head.

"Fuck if I know," she said. "I'm not the mothering type at all."

"I know, love." Trevor slung an arm around her shoulders. "Let's finish this up and we can all go home."

"Yes, please." Tillie looked around to make sure the apartment was clear and then followed the rest out, spelling the lock shut again behind her.

Epilogue

The next night, Mattie found herself at another funeral, a memorial for the thirty-three mages killed in battle. This funeral, while sadder than the fake one for Tillie, was more to her taste – a happy hour celebration of life. With fried appetizers. She lifted another toasted ravioli to her mouth, taking a big bite. "Holy fuck, I've missed these," she muttered with her mouth full.

"What?" Sister Margaret frowned.

Mattie swallowed. "You can't get toasted ravioli in Portland, you know. Well, you could for a while – there was a food cart that had them. But it closed." She paused, remembering, and turned the rest of her ravioli to dip the unbitten side in marinara. "I heard the guy died. He was really young, actually. Good guy. Made great toasted ravs and played a mean blues guitar."

A silence fell over the group as they thought of others gone too soon.

Trevor lifted his red wine. "To good people who've died too young."

"Hear, hear." Mattie raised her gin and tonic, clinking with Trevor and then Tillie and Sister Margaret as they toasted as well. She sipped the cold drink and set it back down.

"Wait a second, though," said Sister Margaret. "Why can't you get toasted ravioli?"

"It's a St. Louis thing," said Tillie. "You didn't know that?"

The nun shrugged. "I've never been anywhere else."

"That's crazy," said Mattie. "How—"

She broke off as Giovani pulled back the empty chair at their table with a clatter and sat down.

"Thank you for coming," he said.

"Of course," said Mattie. "How are you doing?"

He shook his head. "I can't help but feel responsible for each of these deaths."

"Don't be an idiot," said Sister Margaret. "Every mage involved volunteered. Honor their deaths by acknowledging that they were adults who knew the risk."

Giovani smiled. "You have quite the way with words, Sister."

"Fuckin' A." Sister Margaret punctuated this with a swig of her Budweiser. "So, what's next?"

"What do you mean?" asked Mattie. "Isn't it over now?"

"Not by a long shot," she replied.

"The head of the Auditors is gone," said Giovani. "But the organization's body still lives."

"That's not how it's supposed to work," said Mattie. "What the hell?"

"You can't expect them to just go away overnight," said Trevor. "How many agents are out there?"

"I honestly have no idea," said Giovani. "There must be thousands of them, stationed at other quarters around the world or out on assignment."

"And they'll carry out those assignments," finished Tillie.

"Of course," said Giovani. "They have no reason to believe that anything has happened to the Pontiff and the court. They'll bring in or kill their targets, deliver them to the station they were assigned, and then they'll await their next assignment."

"And when the next assignment doesn't come?" Trevor leaned forward.

"A next assignment might still come," said Giovani. "It'll take a while for the effects of what we've done here to actually affect the agents out there." He gestured to the world in general.

"Let's skip ahead," suggested Sister Margaret. "What happens when the assignments stop coming in? When people who are expecting to hear from the Pontiff or the court don't hear from them and can't get ahold of them?"

"I have no idea," Giovani admitted again.

"Okay, then," said Tillie. "So we have some time to figure it out."

Nicole dropped into an empty chair beside Tillie. "There's also the question of who ratted us out to the court."

"Shezza," said Tillie with conviction. "It had to be Agent Shezza."

Giovani shook his head. "It may be. But Agent Shezza is among those we mourn today, so if it was her, we may never know."

"Damn," said Tillie. "She died getting those kids out?"

"I assume so," said Nicole. "She didn't come out and the last of the children to come out are being treated for burns right now. I have to assume she somehow sacrificed herself to make sure every last one made it."

Another moment of silence fell and Trevor silently held up his glass in another toast. The group followed suit, sipping with gravitas.

"What's our end goal?" asked Mattie after a beat. She took another sip of her gin and tonic. "When are we done?"

"We might never be done," said Giovani. "Or at least I might not. You know, we talked about giving my life a purpose. This is it for me, for the foreseeable future. You, on the other hand, are free to disengage at any time. As the good sister pointed out, you're all volunteers."

"I'm in for the long haul," said Tillie. "I'm officially dead anyway."

"I go where Tillie goes," said Trevor.

"These bastards pissed me off," said Sister Margaret. "I'm in as long as Sister Catherine lets me."

Four faces peered at Mattie expectantly.

"Fuck it," she said. "Me too."

About the Author

Anna McCluskey writes humorous contemporary and urban fantasy. When she isn't writing, you can find her hiking around Oregon with her partner and their dog, Chalupa. Or, if it's raining, snuggled up under a blanket with Chalupa or a kitty, drinking a ridiculous amount of tea.

For information on upcoming projects, check out her website, **www.theannafiles.com**.